RUTHLESS HEIR

STREET KINGS
BOOK FOUR

SIENNA SNOW

STREET KINGS BOOK 4

RUTHLESS
HEIR

Sienna Snow

Copyright Page

Cover Design: Steamy Designs

Editor: Jennifer Haymore

www.siennasnow.com

ISBN - eBook - 978-1-948756-28-0

ISBN - Print - 978-1-948756-29-7

ISBN - Special Edition - 979-8-88535-014-3

1

THREE WEEKS AGO

Devani

"WE CAN'T DO THIS ANYMORE."

I kept quiet and stared at the intricately designed ceiling with its multitude of patterns in gray and silver. My heartbeat drummed in my chest as my breath and body calmed from the activities of only moments ago.

"Are you listening to me?"

I swallowed the lump forming in my throat and the ache growing in the pit of my stomach. For over a month and a half, I'd waited for this conversation to come. Then, the second my foot had slipped through the hidden passageway leading into the penthouse, something told me tonight was the night.

I shouldn't have come here in the first place. I said this to myself every time I snuck inside his building.

But, he drew me as a butterfly sought nectar.

I was the Queen of Diamonds, the one without emotions, whose blood ran as cold as the jewels in the many mines I owned. Instead, I used logic and calculation in every aspect of my life.

I was a master chess player, strategizing, exploiting, and utilizing every asset in my arsenal to achieve my end goal.

I'd coined and owned the name "manipulative bitch."

My petite size was one of my greatest advantages. No one knew when I'd strike or if I felt anything while making a kill.

At thirteen, I'd learned one of the keys to surviving the game, and I lived by it religiously: Never let anyone matter.

Until him.

Samir Krishan King.

Why had I let him in? Why had I fucking broken every one of my damn rules?

I knew better, for fuck's sake. I was one of the directors for Solon North America, an underground organization tasked with using any means necessary to stop human trafficking worldwide.

I hadn't even crawled out of the hole of cleaning up the mess from one of my best agents seeking her happily ever after. And now, I had to face the consequences of my mistake and pay the price.

"Don't ignore me, Devani." Sam leaned over me, his

deep amber eyes boring into mine and reigniting the arousal he coaxed to life with his mere presence.

The way his pupils dilated until his irises became rings of gold told me he felt it too. However, just as fast, he reined it in, and a crease formed between his brows.

If he only knew I found him more attractive when he scowled.

He'd taken my breath away from that very first meeting so many years ago. Every plane of his handsome face appeared as if a sculptor had precisely designed it. Then there was how he carried himself that made a person stop to look deeper. It was a mixture of sheer confidence, the aura of danger, and the intensity with which he studied everyone around him, friend or foe.

"I couldn't ignore you even if I tried." I resisted the urge to run a finger down the dark shadow of stubble covering his jaw and seduce him into pushing this conversation off for another time.

"Acknowledging my words would be nice."

But as always, changing Sam's mind was like trying to move a mountain.

"What is it you expect me to say?" I wrapped my legs around his waist, shifted my hips, and flipped him onto his back.

He countered just as fast, grabbing hold of my arms and pinning them to the hollow of my back. We both knew I could break free if I wanted.

Except I wouldn't.

Anger radiated from his golden gaze. "You keep coming

back to my bed. Yet you're planning to marry another man."

Guilt and shame coursed through my heart and mind. This man knew who I was, the good, the bad, the ugly, and the unforgivable.

"Maybe." I looked away, hating the charade I'd have to play to reach my goals.

It was the only way. I had to make everyone believe, to make Sam believe.

He'd never understand why I'd agreed to this and betrayed him.

Why would the notorious Devani Patel, the Queen of Diamonds, allow herself to become another man's arm candy? Why would she walk into a den of diseased vipers and let them believe she would become their saving grace?

He'd never know that I'd sacrifice everything to give him the one thing he'd never admit wanting. The one thing he dreamed of, the one thing that, if he carried out, would destroy the empire he'd built.

But the answer was simple.

Revenge.

Revenge for so many people, but especially for him.

Sam's grip tightened. "Bullshit."

"Nothing...nothing is set in stone, Sam."

"What are you hiding?"

I smirked. "Many things. That's my job."

"Are you saying tonight you came here for a last fuck before you walk into another bastard's bed?"

"You know damn well it's not like that between us. We don't just fuck." I couldn't hide my raw emotions.

This connection we had went deeper than the physical. He knew it. I knew it. Well, I thought he knew it.

Maybe it was better he felt this way. I'd never said the words, even though they burned on the tip of my tongue.

Saying them would change everything, and neither of us was ready for the consequences.

No, that wasn't the truth. I couldn't risk it.

How had something that started as a one-night stand after a poker game become something neither of us could label but left us raw and exposed?

This was taboo according to where we were in society. I was the diamond mogul from the world of the polished elite. He was one of the notorious billionaire King Brothers who dealt in favors and lived between the legitimate world and organized crime. If only our paths had never crossed, I wouldn't have challenged him to that poker game, and we'd never have become lovers.

One of his hands slid up my back, threaded into my hair, and drew my face to his. "No, I don't. We fuck when it's convenient. We have a good time. No strings, no commitments. Weren't those the rules?"

"Sam—" My lips trembled for a split second before I harnessed my emotions.

"No. I don't want to hear it."

"I don't want it like this between us."

"How the fuck did you expect it to go? We aren't in some from-lovers-to-friends situation. You're stepping into a life you said you despised, into a life you swore you would never live, into that asshole's world."

That asshole being Ashok Shah. Sam's biological father, the man who'd abandoned Sam's pregnant mother, Veda Kumari, for a lucrative marriage to an heiress.

How could I tell him the road I was following would save him and countless others? I'd rather Sam hated me than let the monsters like Ashok Shah roam free.

And I planned to take down not only Shah but a whole organization, which included three other men—my uncles. They'd destroyed a little girl's childhood, sent her off to boarding school, and then played Monopoly with her inheritance.

"I never wanted to hurt you."

"Did you forget that Sam King doesn't have a heart? You can't hurt me. I'll be fine." He released me and rolled me to his side as he shifted and rose from the bed.

As he reached the doors leading out of his bedroom, he said over his shoulder, "Don't come back, Devani. What we had is over. You're moving on. I'll take your cue and do the same."

I closed my eyes and nodded.

Ending things was for the best. Though one thing would never happen.

There was no moving on from Samir Krishan King.

<hr>

PRESENT DAY

. . .

"LADIES AND GENTLEMEN, YOU HAVE YOUR ASSIGNMENTS." I studied my team, feeling the weight of what would become my last mission as Lead Director of Solon North America.

After over a year of planning, everything sat on the precipice of activation. No going back now.

Whatever the outcome, one thing remained the same.

I'd go down in flames or die trying. I planned to take every risk necessary to reach my end goal.

Get my revenge and complete my last mission—ever.

I had nothing to lose.

I hadn't earned the reputation for being a manipulative fucking bitch for nothing.

"As of now," I continued, "we are on active. We will regroup in a week at a location relayed via our network."

"When will we receive our security clearances?" Jesika Rawal, a field operative, asked.

In her non-Solon life, she was a managing partner of a well-known New York law firm and the daughter of an Indian-American venture capitalist.

We ran in the same social circles, and she would be my eyes and ears from the periphery for any necessary intel.

And based on the gossip sites and rumor mills, she was Sam's new lover. I'd seen firsthand several events they'd attended together. Striking was an understatement to describe them when they entered a room: tall, stylish, and rebellious in a world where rules and expectations were the norm. Then there was the chemistry between them.

They laughed together, genuinely enjoyed each other's company, and no one could doubt their relationship went beyond sex.

I never begrudged any of my agents taking lovers. We all had them, but Jesika with Sam...

Just the thought of it brought bile to my throat.

"With the high-profile level of the case and the need for increased security," Noah Carter, one of my field leads, answered, snapping me out of my thoughts, "each of you has a different security protocol that we will monitor using a trusted outside vendor. She is the best of the best."

I'd trained Noah when he'd first come into the game as a green eighteen-year-old, who couldn't believe someone the same age as him was his superior officer and could lay him on his ass if he got out of line. He understood me as a person and accepted all of my quirks, as a boss and a friend. Plus, I trusted him with my life. He'd head up my ground crew and cover my ass if I ever ended up in a situation where I needed extraction.

"And the equipment we are using? Can we trust it?" Tasha Lee, another of my team, probed.

"The equipment we are using is from one of our own, a former agent, now a freelance developer." This time my partner and future replacement, Neil Joshi, spoke. "Director Patel, Agent Carter, and I know her well. There isn't anyone else we would trust with devices for this assignment."

Neil's gaze flickered toward me for a second and then back to Tasha.

"Are there any more questions?" I scanned the room, holding each team member's eyes for a second before moving on to the next.

When everyone remained quiet, I said, "As I stated a few moments ago, we are now active. Continue normal daily operation and training while you await location and placement. Thank you, ladies and gentlemen."

Slowly, the room cleared, with the exception of Neil and Noah. The two men remained quiet until we were alone and the door closed.

I'd expected this—the bad cop, worse cop routine.

If they weren't the closest people I had to brothers, I'd punch them in the face for overstepping their positions.

"Stop glaring at me and say what you two need to get off your chests."

"We don't have to do this, Devani. You don't have to play the sacrificial lamb." Neil rose from his seat and leaned against the now closed door.

This was his signature move to ensure no one could return to the room and accidentally interrupt a conversation.

"Of course, I do. I won't let any of the fuckers win. Do you think my uncles, your father, Ashok Shah, or their friends should get away with what they have done?"

Neil was my original partner at Solon over fifteen years ago. And we'd worked countless cases together since. However, my unconventional and extremely underaged start in the organization had given me a bit of seniority over him.

We'd both climbed through the ranks at an unheard-of speed with the same mission in mind.

To take down our families.

His was to destroy his father, Arun Joshi, and brother, Lukesh. They'd taken the real estate empire his grandfather had built and turned it into an organization to fund various illegal businesses, including human trafficking.

Mine wasn't so virtuous as Neil's.

All I wanted was to take down the uncles I knew were involved in the deaths of my parents and brother. Deaths I couldn't prove were murders.

My grandfather had offered all four of his sons the option of gaining their inheritance early through cash or later in the form of equal shares in the company. My uncles took the money, and Papa inherited the entire company.

When Papa found diamonds and rare gem veins on land he'd purchased through the company, my uncles regretted their decision and wanted back in. And the rest was history. My parents and brother lost their lives, I became an orphan, and my uncles squandered my inheritance.

"Cut the bullshit." Noah propped his feet on the table. "This is us. We know the truth, even if you don't want to admit it."

I lifted a brow. "Elaborate, then."

"This is about more than destroying the Circle of Ten."

If they only knew. By taking down the Circle of Ten, I could accomplish my main objective.

The Circle was an underground network of men going

back over thirty-five years. This group of men had met in England during their university years and decided to join forces. They used their connections to assist each other in various ways to further their agendas, everything from money laundering to their most lucrative endeavor, human trafficking.

We'd managed to identify nine out of the ten members. Somewhere at the top of the hierarchy stood Joshi and Shah, followed by three European aristocrats from old families. What their true roles were, we hadn't quite narrowed down yet. Then there were my fucking uncles. In my opinion, they couldn't be more than errand boys at most, but who knew?

The last seat had belonged to Neil's brother, Lukesh Joshi. The supposed heir apparent to the Circle. We learned Joshi had made room for Luke by disposing of an original member whom he no longer found useful.

Too bad Luke would never lead the Circle or occupy his seat ever again. Well, unless someone wanted to scuba dive in the international waters off the coast of Florida, collect any remains the sea life hadn't consumed, and pile them in a chair at their next meeting.

With Lukesh Joshi out of the picture, the count for the demise of the Circle was one down and nine more to go.

"Since you know so much, tell me. What else is it about?"

Neil answered in an angry, hard tone. "It's about Sam King."

"Sam and I fucked when we got the itch. After that,

there was nothing more to it." I kept my words emotionless.

I'd kept my relationship with Sam as private as possible. And the select few who knew anything about us thought of us as a fuckbuddies situation.

"I call bullshit, again." Noah stood, bracing his hands on the table, the relaxed demeanor from earlier completely gone. "You trained me. I learned every fucking thing about manipulating from you. Don't think I can't see what's happening."

"Since you've figured it out, keep going."

"This case goes deeper than our assignments and taking down your corrupt family. You're avenging what happened to Sam King."

"Ashok Shah is the top player in this game. If he goes down, all the cards fall. Destroying him won't fix the damage he did to his son."

It may not fix the damage, but it might give him some semblance of peace.

"Are you saying this last case has nothing to do with your personal relationship with Sam King?" Neil stared at me in the hard, no-nonsense way he used when interrogating suspects.

I almost snorted. The tough-guy act never worked on me.

In Solon, he went by the name Extractor for the many unique methods in his arsenal for acquiring cooperation from suspects.

"Correct," I said, without blinking an eye, and then

added, "And for the record, there is no relationship with Sam. Once upon a time, we fucked. For the safety of all on this case, it won't happen again."

"You've gotten so good at lying that I think you almost believe your lies." Neil shook his head. "But I've known you long enough to see past that cool, manipulative Queen of Diamonds facade."

My temper flared, but I tamped it down. "What is it that you see?"

"You walked away because you did the very thing Lilly Lennox, now Lilly King, did with the older King brother."

"You're trying to make it into something it wasn't."

"Am I?" Neil countered. "Someone else can replace you."

"The operation won't work without me, and you know it. I'm the prize on your father's pedestal of society. You come home with the Queen of Diamonds as your woman, and he will give you your brother's seat at the table with the Circle of Ten."

"It's settled, then," Noah stated with a tone of resignation in his words. "It won't be a problem for the two of you to pose as a couple and possibly marry if it means completing the assignment."

I cocked a hand on my hip. "We established this."

"So it won't bother you when King is in the same room with Jesika?"

I kept my features thoroughly schooled and my emotions locked down. "Why would it?"

"Okay, then." Noah shook his head. "Nothing we say

will change your mind about this, and you set this whole thing up as if you're about to go out in a blaze of glory."

Noah had no idea how right he was.

I let my lips curve at the corners. "That's my standard operating protocol. Go big or go home."

2

SAM

"WANT TO EXPLAIN THE REASON FOR OUR UNITED
appearance at this fundraiser again?" I glanced at my eldest
brother, Nik, who sat across from me in our limo.

"Because we are making a point to certain factions of
society that the Kings are no longer in the shadows."

A slow pulse of annoyance ignited on the sides of my
head, knowing I had a long night ahead of me.

"You're such a dick."

"We all are. You just hide your ruthlessness under those
ten-thousand-dollar suits. I'm more upfront about it."

I couldn't argue with Nik's observation. We were two
of the four notorious King brothers of New York City,
with Kir and Rey making up the other two. Our rags-to-
riches story always piqued media interest: boys from the

streets adopted by Arin King and then turned into real estate tycoons.

However, it was our real business, our underground business, that kept things rolling in a city where certain factions of society could never meet but required a middleman to conduct business.

The role of intermediaries was where my brothers and I came in. We bridged the gap between the elite and the unsavory. We made the introductions and brokered the deals.

Of course, all of it came for a fee—a fee paid in favors, collected at a time of our choosing.

We had a unique place in the world, the ability to move seamlessly from one society to another. Me more so than my brothers.

I was the polished one. The Columbia graduate. The face of King Holdings, the legitimate aspect of our family business. Well, as legitimate as the other fuckers who were born into the upper crust acting as if their shit smelled like roses.

I picked up my tumbler of scotch, sipped, and then said, "Sometimes you have to play the game before you go in for the kill. If I didn't deal the way I do, we wouldn't have the new acquisition in our portfolio netting us a hefty profit."

"Speaking of." Nik lifted his glass and gestured to the building coming into view as the car rolled to a stop in the driveway of the Carina Hotel in Manhattan.

The Carina was one of the many hotels under the Argo

Hotel and Real Estate Group, the conglomerate I'd mentioned acquiring a few seconds ago.

"This is some property. It's going to piss certain people off that we are now in the hotel business." Nik smirked.

"We've always had our hand in the hotel business. The Carina and its sister locations are only the first in New York. And if our family ventures threaten people, that has nothing to do with us. Business is business. I don't make decisions based on personal feelings."

I'd learned long ago to set emotions to the back of my mind and use cold, hard logic when taking any course of action.

"Shah won't view it as anything but personal."

I clenched my jaw. I hated thinking about the piece of shit who'd abandoned and then murdered my mother.

Wasn't it enough that I fucking saw a resemblance to the fucker in the mirror every damn morning?

With how high-profile my life was, it always made me wonder how the hell no one noticed how much we looked alike.

"New York real estate is about who has the means and the ability to deal and to move the fastest. There are always multiple players around any card table. If he lost sight of his competition, that's his problem."

"You want me to believe you don't enjoy the fact you stuck it to him while making us richer?"

I smirked. "There are always benefits to being the true bastard of the King brothers. Sometimes I get lucky and can take something from the fucker who made me a bastard."

"Since you brought up the bastard bit—" Nik's eyes narrowed, "—we need to discuss the will."

Fuck. The night was just getting better and better.

The last thing I wanted to discuss was the will of my biological grandmother, Ashok Shah's mother. Sara Shah had left everything to her grandchildren, specifying the eldest as the heir to the majority of the billion-dollar Shah fortune. A fortune Ashok Shah stole when he filed a false will upon Sara's death.

Why hadn't I taken my own damn car and met everyone at the event?

Because I'd probably have skipped the whole thing, and Nik knew it.

"I want nothing to do with the will or the money. My net worth is more than all of you fuckers."

Only one person could put all of us to shame. The reason I'd rather have spent the evening monitoring the underground poker club I owned with my brothers than attending this fucking fundraiser.

"It's not just about you. Danika and Jayna deserve their inheritance."

Of course, he'd hit me in the one place I was the weakest. Danika and Jayna.

Not only had they married into the King family, but Danika was also Nik's wife, and Jayna made Kir a less piss-and-vinegar version of himself. The two women were my only living biological family. Well, the ones who I claimed and claimed me back.

Danika was the daughter of Ashok Shah's sister, Reka. A sister he'd disowned for not following tradition. And Jayna was my half-sister, the daughter of Monica Shah, the heiress the asshole had thrown my pregnant mother aside to marry.

Nik damn well knew I'd do anything for Danika and Jayna, but those two never needed anyone to play interference for them. They wouldn't have any problem holding a knife to my throat to get my attention.

"Why aren't they coming to me about it? Neither of them would appreciate you playing messenger boy for them. Tell me I'm wrong."

A flicker of annoyance passed over his face. Good. He deserved that.

"Let's say this is a warning before they strike. Something is brewing in Shah's world, and the ladies have decided it's time to act."

"Are you saying my sisters are going to force my hand?"

Even though Danika was my cousin in the family-tree way, I viewed her no different than Jayna. I'd fight the world for her, and without hesitation, I knew she'd do the same for me. Danika, Jayna, and I had an unbreakable bond we could have only dreamed about as kids.

"They share your blood. What do you think?"

"Taking on Shah is dangerous, especially now that Danika is pregnant. You can't risk him targeting her."

"First of all, if you think it's even remotely possible to

keep my wife in any form of a protective cage, you don't know anything about her." The humor in Nik's tone lightened my irritation with the whole subject matter. "Second, dealing with your history is part of life. And the only way you'll ever move past what happened to your mother is by toppling Shah's house of cards."

"Destroying Shah isn't something I give two shits about. It won't bring back my mother. Veda Kumari's blood covers everything Shah has. Hell, it's soaked in Kir, Rey, and your parents' blood too."

Nik sighed. "I hear you. Before I let it drop, answer this question."

I waited for him to continue.

"What would it take for you to go after Shah?"

"It won't happen. Danika and Jayna are safe."

"So he'd have to go after someone you love?"

My mind drifted to the stories Danika and Jayna had told me about their lives growing up under Shah's roof. About the abuse they and Monica Shah suffered almost daily until they'd finally escaped.

"As long as Shah stays in his corner away from all of us, especially those I call mine, I don't give a shit what he does. And since he knows we have the original will and he likes his nice life, we have nothing to worry about."

Maybe my words were a bit archaic, but Shah liked to hurt the women in my life. He'd taken my mother from me, abused Jayna and her mother to the point they would have sold their souls to the devil to escape him, and kept Danika under such a controlling hand that she had allowed herself to become a puppet to create some semblance of a life.

I'd destroy him before he added another one to his list.

"And if he crosses the line?"

I narrowed my gaze at Nik. The asshole was testing me.

"If it came to that, under all this polish and grooming of the upper crust, I still have every one of those skills Arin forced me to perfect as part of my arsenal."

When it came to fathers, my adoptive father was anything but typical. Each brother had a set curriculum to learn. However, since I was the youngest of the brothers, Arin had the most influence on my education. From the beginning, he planned for my role in elite circles and expected me to learn weapons and skills no one could detect. I doubted many people could say they grew up with trainers for the proper weapon, fighting, and defense skills and techniques mixed in with tutors in physics and calculus.

God, I missed Arin. The man believed in me even when I fucked up, and he never gave up on me.

"Good to hear. Got worried you were going soft."

"Asshole." Then again, I was in the car with Arin's replica. The man who'd kept us a unit as we ran the streets of New York as dumb kids. "Do me a favor. If I promise to keep an open mind when Dani and Jay come at me with their plan, will you drop the subject for the rest of the night?"

"I'll drop it, but I make no promises from the ladies."

"I guess that is as good as I'll get."

"Speaking of ladies. Has security given their ETA?" I checked my watch.

"Arrived ten minutes ago." Nik poured another serving of scotch for himself and offered the bottle to me, but I shook my head. "They are waiting for us with Kir and your lovely date inside."

My mind shifted to Jesika Rawal, someone who many believed was my current lover but was only a friend and my informant for all things high society. In exchange, I helped her funnel her inheritance into untraceable accounts.

We used each other for our own purposes, keeping our reasons for what we did to ourselves.

She was also Solon. She knew I knew, but we'd never openly spoken about it. I'd spent years with the best in the game. Now it was child's play spotting them. Plus, Kir had let it slip that he planned to meet with his Solon contact, Jes, once, and I'd put two and two together.

"Since the Shah subject is closed, I want to ask you about something else."

"Go ahead. Whatever it is, it can't be any worse than the Shah subject."

The smirk on Nik's face made it seem like I'd just thrown down a challenge, and he'd taken up the gauntlet. "It's been a while since you've seen her. Are you ready to be in the same room with your Queen of Diamonds? Especially if the rumors are true and she is on her way to marrying the Joshi prince."

"You really are a dick."

3

DEVANI

"REMEMBER, EVERYTHING SPOKEN FROM THIS POINT ON IS recorded," I muttered as I approached Neil.

He stood next to his father, Arun Joshi, and Ashok Shah as they engaged in an animated conversation.

The knowledge Sam was Jesika's date for tonight sat heavy in my stomach. When he'd said he planned to move on, I knew it would happen. I'd prepared myself. I hadn't expected it to be within days of our last time together and not with someone from my world, someone I worked with closely.

I had to remember I'd done this to myself.

Focus on the end goal.

Everything was about the end goal.

Save Sam. Eliminate the Circle of Ten. Protect all those

women and children, then get out.

I could do this, no matter how much it hurt.

I scanned the area and noticed neither Neil's mother, Smita, nor his thirteen-year-old sister, Mia, were with the group.

This was just great. The two decent members of the family were nowhere around.

I adored Smita Joshi. Something about the former Bollywood actress and model made me want to protect her and hide her away. She still radiated a regal beauty beyond her years, as well as an aura of fragility.

Neil had told me his father had barely spoken or engaged with his mother after Mia's birth. They lived completely separate lives and only came out in public as a couple for functions. Joshi had expected all of his children to be male, and having a female lowered his stock.

In fact, Neil's mother and sister lived in a house he'd built for them and not in one of the many properties under the Joshi portfolio.

I'd hoped tonight would have been one evening where I could spend some time with the ladies. Their presence would have allowed me to move about more freely.

Oh, well. I guessed I'd have to play arm candy.

I stepped in next to Neil, and Arun Joshi's face lit up in a calculating way that seemed way too friendly for a potential father-in-law.

The fucker honestly thought he'd won the lottery with me.

Yep, that's what I was. Every-fucking-body's golden

ticket. I'd burn it all to the ground before producing the next generation for any of these fuckers.

God. I sounded bitchy as hell.

Poor little rich girl. No parents. No one to love her but literal mines and mines of jewels.

Okay, enough pity-partying. Focus, asshole.

"Ahh. There you are, Devani," Ashok Shah said in Gujarati, the native language from India spoken in both of our family homes.

His eyes lit up as he scanned me in a way that made me want to throat-punch him. What was with these two?

"Neil, you are a lucky man to have such a jewel on your arm." Shah winked at Neil.

Oh, for fuck's sake.

"I am. Devani is more than a prize to show off. She is the head of her family's company. After she took over the management, profits increased exponentially."

"Maybe one day you can assist Neil with our enterprise in the same manner." Shah and Arun Joshi nodded to each other.

It was almost on the tip of my tongue to ask which enterprise he meant, the one the public knew about, or the underground one used to aid the kidnapping of girls.

Instead of saying anything, I gave a noncommittal shrug.

"I was just telling everyone about the deal you made with Jayna to excavate the diamond pipe on our property in Botswana. Because of that endeavor, we've increased interest in our mineral subsidiaries."

It amazed me how men like Ashok Shah rewrote

history.

He'd thought that he could keep his wealth hidden by transferring his worldwide assets to Jayna when she turned eighteen. And then, he'd tried to force her to marry Joshi's oldest son, Luke, as repayment for Joshi financing the purchase of said assets.

Jayna marrying Kir derailed Shah's agreement with Joshi. So now, Jayna solely owned the diamond pipe and all the profits that came with it.

"Jayna is a hard negotiator. But in the end, we both came to a place where our companies benefitted." I glanced in the direction where Jayna stood with Kir.

As per her reputation for pushing fashion, Jayna wore a one-shoulder gown seemingly held together by giant safety pins on the sides until it reached her waist. Beside her, Kir's custom tuxedo should have looked too formal and drab. Instead, his clothing choice gave him a sophisticated and dangerous vibe, especially with the slight hints of the tattoos peeking up along the column of his neck and clear as day on his hands.

"Jayna is smart and knows business," Arun added to the conversation. *"It's a family trait. Wouldn't you agree?"*

I'd leave this all to Neil. Complimenting Shah was where I drew the line.

On cue, Neil jumped in. *"You're absolutely right. You and Auntie Monica did a fine job with her education."*

Shah's jaw hardened for a second at the mention of his ex-wife, then eased. *"Yes, my daughter is brilliant. Too bad I couldn't influence her to make a better match when it came to marriage."* He shook his head as if he had failed. *"I guess I can't win all the fights. If only the Father above had given me more children. Perhaps a son. Then my legacy would live on."*

Everything inside me heated, rapidly growing to a raging boil.

He had a son. A son he'd thrown away.

Arun patted Shah on the back. *"Neil will carry on our legacy, my friend. He is as much your son as he is mine. And once these two make it official, I'm sure they will produce more than enough children for both of us to spoil."*

I shot Neil a mock glare, but his eyes took on a hard edge I hadn't expected. I'd always known he hated his father, but the venom he flashed toward Shah surprised me.

I laughed, giving him a joking jab. *"I have to get him to propose first. I think we still have some time yet."*

"On that note, I think we should get a drink." Neil steered me toward a server with a tray of champagne flutes.

"Want to tell me what that look was all about?" I asked under my breath in English.

Neil grabbed two flutes, handing one to me. "Nothing, really. These evenings are becoming mundane. It's the same old song and dance every few days."

I wanted to call him out on sidestepping my question but decided to let it go. "All they care about is us shagging and making babies."

He smirked. "I saw your face when Shah made his son comment. The flames in your eyes looked lethal. You may want to keep that under wraps."

"You only know my tells because we trained together. No one else can figure out shit about me. Cold as the diamonds in my mines, remember?"

"Why do you play that up so much? You'd have a hell of a lot more friends if you thawed a little."

"I have friends. I'm selective, that's all."

"Yes. Yes. Separation of church and state. Where do I fall into this?"

"Besides my replacement?"

"Yes."

"Family. The one I picked. Although, it sucks that we have to pretend we are hopelessly into each other." I gave him a flirty smile. "This is seriously bordering on ince—"

My thoughts drifted away as my eyes connected with rich amber ones. Everything inside me clenched, and my heartbeat accelerated.

Fuck.

The man I couldn't have. The man I couldn't let go.

The pain, the need, the longing of the last few weeks roared to life.

God. He took my breath away.

Where his brothers gave the edge of danger when they polished up, telling the world they were outsiders among them, Samir King was the actual dangerous one, the most ruthless, the one who seamlessly blended in. His chiseled good looks and tailored clothing gave him an aura of refined elegance. Then, when someone looked deeper into those mesmerizing eyes, there was no mistaking the intelligence taking in every detail of every situation.

The desperate need to touch him pulled at every fiber of my being. The ache, almost visceral and unexplainable, burned in my chest. It had been like this from the beginning with us.

No matter where we were in a room, the draw made us seek each other out.

Sam continued to stare at me. The pulse of energy between us charged deep into my soul. Logic screamed for me to look away. Too much teetered on the edge.

As sense finally penetrated my mind, I refocused on Neil. "What was I saying?"

"You were about to call what we are doing incest."

I released a deep breath as I realized everything that had passed between Sam and me had happened within mere seconds.

"You have to admit it's a bit messed up."

"Yeah, well, we shouldn't have joined the circus if we didn't want to have weird shit happen to us."

My phone beeped, saving me from responding and giving me the cue to move to the hotel lounge to pick up some microchips from my favorite hacker.

"Time to go powder my nose and grab a new shade of lipstick."

I walked into the private lounge I'd received as the meeting location for the rendezvous with the Little Rabbit, aka Danika King. Who also happened to be my closest friend. In the last year and a half, though, I'd taken a more cautious approach to our friendship for both our sakes.

She'd married into the King family, and as far as the world knew, Danika and I were socialite enemies. A rivalry due to some made-up bullshit from our teens that never happened, as far as we could recall.

Sometimes I wished things were simple again between us. When Danika pretended to be the poor Shah relation by day and hacker extraordinaire for hire by night. And I was the ambitious Solon agent trying to climb the Solon leadership ladder.

Long before I knew she was the Little Rabbit, a legendary underground hacker wanted on six continents for her vigilante ways. Though most people thought she belonged to the male persuasion. Because, of course, only people with penises had the brains to hack and be badasses.

I could admit that when I'd learned she'd kept her secret identity as the Little Rabbit from me, I'd wanted to punch her in the nose.

I was her ride-or-die, the person who taught her how to protect herself, and she'd kept that shit from me. Finally, after I'd calmed the fuck down, I understood her reasoning.

We all had our demons and secrets.

I was definitely no saint when it came to mine.

I could admit that I had gotten an IOU out of her for the incident. One I had yet to collect. I wasn't sure if I'd ever collect.

She was the best in her field. To describe her skills as dangerous when given a laptop was an understatement. But she wasn't an agent, no matter how much time I'd spent making sure she could take care of herself. Plus, she had a baby on the way, and I couldn't risk her safety.

She'd given up her revenge against Shah for the new life she had today, for Nik.

Never would I bring her into the thick of it.

I scanned the room, taking in every inch of the space. Then, listening to airflow in the area, I gauged for changes in sound aside from the air-conditioning system. A slight whistle in the corner told me a hidden panel or door sat somewhere in that space.

Cheeky girl.

She should know by now that I could find every secret passage in a place. Hell, they were my specialty. Tiny spaces allowed me to discover all the secrets the big fuckers could never learn.

People loved to underestimate my five-foot-two height, thinking my size made me less than or weak. Fools, all of them.

More times than not, my petite stature allowed me to slide in and out of places without leaving a footprint or detection. Something paramount in the spy game.

Plus, it helped I had no issues with claustrophobia or moving about in dark spaces.

I waited another minute in the middle of the room, locked the lounge door from the inside, and then made my way to the corner.

I traced along the wall and found a small groove concealing a lever. Just as I tugged the handle and the panel shifted, a hand grabbed hold of my wrist, pulling me into darkness and pinning me to the wall.

Instinct fired to life, and I shifted my hips, readying to nail the fucker in the balls as I reached for the gun strapped to my thigh. Stilling just as fast, I reined in my need to fight, closed my eyes, and dropped my head against the wall.

"Sam, you shouldn't be here."

"Yes, or no?" Sam asked in that deep rasp that made my body instantly react.

He planned to do to me exactly what I'd done to him time and time again throughout the last few years. He'd never know where I'd pop up to have my way with him. We'd end up fucking in stairwells, closets, pantries, and my favorite—hidden rooms. Then we'd return to whatever event we were attending as if nothing had happened between us.

My breath grew unsteady as my nipples pebbled and arousal pooled between my legs. I shouldn't want him like this, ache for him like this.

A few words, a look, the scent of him, his sheer presence.

"You're with someone else."

"That's not what I asked you." He glided his hand over my throat, down my neck, and skimmed over my breast, moving lower until he cupped the mound of my sex through my dress. "Does he make you come, Highness?"

32

Only Sam had ever called me by that name. It was his way of reminding me of our different stations in life and the fact he believed I was lowering myself with him.

If only he'd known *I* was the one tainted. He'd forged himself out of fire and hardship. While I had more blood on my hands than anyone would believe.

And I planned to add to it without any guilt.

"Nothing to say?" Sam pressed down, then stroked two fingers over my clit, causing the ache deep in my pussy to grow more needy and painful.

Without thought, I lifted against his questing palm, needing the friction I craved, and whispered, "He doesn't touch me at all."

"Am I supposed to believe that you left me for a man who doesn't please you?"

He lowered to his knees and slowly gathered the silken material of my gown up until he had it bunched at my thighs just above where my gun sat strapped against me. Goose bumps prickled over me as cool air glided over my heated skin.

"Never leave home without it, do you?"

"A girl can never be too careful."

"Do you think you're safe now?" His lips brushed the area just shy of my underwear. "I wouldn't be so sure."

"You don't scare me."

He pushed my dress farther up and blew against the silk covering my arousal-soaked clit.

Oh God, I needed more.

Next, his tongue stroked the swollen bundle of nerves,

dampening the material further and rocketing my desire higher.

A whimper escaped my lips as I gripped Sam's shoulders, desperate to hold on to something. The complete darkness in the room drove every sensation to an even more intense level.

"I didn't give you permission to touch me. Put your hands back on the wall."

An ache burned deep and hot inside me. Only he knew this side of me. But I couldn't go there, or I wouldn't survive my plans. I'd created this void between us, and this was the price.

My fingers dug into the jacket of his tuxedo. "I don't need permission. I do what I like."

"Wrong." He stood, grasping my wrists and pressing them above my head.

He brought his mouth a hairsbreadth from mine.

"You lost that right when you chose someone else." Anger radiated through his words. "When you chose an easier life. Now you get what I give you."

I couldn't defend myself. I'd broken our hearts.

"And what is it you plan to give me?"

"First, you answer yes or no."

"You know what I'll say."

"Do I, Highness?"

"Sam, you know me better than anyone else."

"I thought I did. I was wrong. Now answer, yes or no."

"Yes. Dammit. Yes."

He shifted my wrists to one of his hands. Then, using

the other, he cupped my throat, applying enough pressure to make it deliciously uncomfortable and arousing without restricting my airflow.

I couldn't help but moan, loving the feel of him so close to me. All my senses ran on hyperdrive, my body begging for more, needing more, oh so much more.

As if hearing my thoughts, Sam rubbed the stubble along his jaw against my cheek a second before he bit my lower lip, making me gasp.

"Do you ache, Highness? Do you need me to push you? Force you to release that control?"

My core clenched as my pulse jumped. "I took care of myself before you. I am capable of doing it now."

"Don't even pretend for a moment that you don't want more from me." Now he nipped my earlobe. "For three years, I've fucked you in every way possible. I've heard every one of your moans and pleas. I know exactly how to make you beg."

He was too damn cocky for his own good.

To hell with this guilt bogging me down. Right now, I would get laid the way I liked.

Turning my head and lifting up on tiptoes, I took hold of his bottom lip with my teeth and bit down hard enough to draw blood, then licked it.

A growl erupted from his throat a second before he released my wrist, grasped the back of my head, and covered my mouth with his.

The taste of him exploded over my senses, intoxicating and consuming.

35

I wanted more, so much more. His tongue dueled against mine in a game of dominance. One we'd played so many times. My breasts swelled, and my nipples strained against the confines of my gown, desperate for his palms to mold, tease, and pinch.

I scored my nails along the back of his neck, knowing he'd have my marks on his skin, and then dug my fingers into his thick hair.

"Naked. Now." In a frenzy, I pushed at his jacket, needing to get to his skin.

I fucking loved the body he hid under his custom-tailored suits. Not only was he beautiful to look at with his tattooed, sculpted physique, but he moved like a honed weapon.

For someone like me, a man who trained in the muck with his men and could take care of himself was a greater turn-on than any supermodel or movie star.

"Next time," he murmured as he lifted me and then repositioned me onto a ledge. One I never would have known was there in the dark.

"I have to be inside you. It's been too fucking long."

"Hurry." I clutched at his shoulders, unable to hide the desperation in my voice.

The sound of his zipper sliding sent a shiver down my spine.

God, I wanted this. Needed this.

With my dress pushed up far enough for him to step between my legs, he gripped my hip with one hand and shifted my thong to the side with the other. The heat from his straining, thick, hard cock teased my aching pussy.

I squirmed as the urge to pull him closer drove at me.

Fuck. This driving desperation had me on the edge of losing my mind.

When his velvety, bulbous head brushed against my dripping opening, it took everything inside me not to beg him to just put me out of my misery.

He'd been my only lover for nearly three years, and going without him for all these weeks seemed like a lifetime.

"God, I missed how wet you get for me." He slid in a fraction and then pulled out, eliciting a whimper from my lips.

That was it. I was taking things into my own hands.

However, before I could do anything, he plunged to the hilt inside me.

"Fuck, Sam," I cried out, not expecting the exquisite sting of discomfort.

I closed my eyes and reveled in the onslaught of sensations cascading through my body. It was almost too much, too overwhelming.

And I never wanted it to stop.

I'd only ever felt this way with him.

He shouldn't have this kind of hold on me. Not someone like me.

I commanded and called the shots. With him, I surrendered too much control.

Pushing those thoughts aside, I wrapped my arms

around Sam's neck and drew him to me. Using that as a cue, he adjusted his hold on my hips, pulled out, and then slammed back in, setting the hard, brutal pace he knew I loved.

My pussy responded, spasming with each plunge of his cock.

He kneaded and massaged my ass, tugging me back and forth into every wicked thrust. I'd undoubtedly have bruises on my hips and back from this vicious pounding. And I'd take all he gave because every inch of me loved it.

"More. I need more."

"I know."

He rolled his hips in that perfect way, hitting all the right spots inside me with each pummeling thrust. My body answered his demands by quickening first with tiny tremors and then clenching around his pistoning shaft.

Heat pooled deep in my core, building higher and higher. My skin burned, and sweat tinged every part of me.

If only I could see his face. I loved watching him. His intensity drove my desire higher.

This was part of the punishment for leaving him.

I had no doubt.

Sex in the dark, where no one could see. To remind me what a horrible woman I was to have kept us in the shadows.

He grabbed my jaw, pulled me out of my thoughts, and brought his lips to mine. "I'm still here."

"Sam," I whispered as my mind clouded with arousal and emotion. "I need you."

"I know. Now come for me." He released my face and slid his finger between our bodies.

It took the barest brush against my clit, and my body erupted, flexing and clamping down on his cock. I rode the torrential waves of euphoria and exhilaration only this man could harvest out of me.

"One more," he ordered before I'd barely come down, catapulting me back up to the crest again.

He grew harder and thicker inside me, the hand on my hip digging in as if he never wanted to let me go.

"Devani," he cried out as he came, bucking his hips into me, riding out his release.

Neither of us spoke as we let our breaths calm, only holding each other. The scent of us lingered in the air, as well as the weight of what we'd just done. I needed him so much and wanted him on a level I shouldn't.

What was I thinking? There were too many consequences for acting irrationally. This man was my weakness, and no one could know this. The problem was that more people than I wanted knew about us.

Sam braced his arms on the ledge on either side of my hips, his semi-hard cock continuing to throb inside me. The need for him still burned deep in my core. It was as if the visceral desire between us hadn't even cooled a minute amount.

I waited for him to speak, expecting whatever he said next to sting.

"When you go back to him, my cum will be deep inside you. It will drip out of you. Will he want to touch you knowing a King has destroyed you, pounded into you, made you come around his cock?"

My core contracted, even knowing he'd used the crude words as a way to hurt me.

"He doesn't touch me. How many times do I need to say this?"

"Yet you chose him." He pulled free of me and brought me down to the floor, and then placed a handkerchief between my legs before he set my thong in place over it.

The intimacy of the things between us left me too raw.

We straightened our clothes in silence, the darkness in the room a perfect cloak for the emotions roiling between us.

Using my senses, I moved toward him. "I have my reasons for what I do."

"Maybe, one day, you'll care to explain them to me." Sam shifted me in the direction of the doorway I'd first entered.

A click sounded, and a panel slid to the side, flooding my eyes with light and forcing me to squint. Once my sight adjusted, I turned to Sam and took him in.

Lip swollen from my bite, face flushed from our hard fuck against the wall, and still gorgeous as ever. However, if anyone caught sight of him, they'd know he'd pursued an activity outside the ballroom.

He had the look of a well-fucked man.

His pupils dilated, and he licked his lips as he scanned my rumpled state.

His response had my heartbeat accelerating and my barely quenched arousal firing to life again.

"You need to either find another dress or figure out a good excuse for the state of that gown."

I glanced down. We'd ruined the dress, and I had no choice but to take the employee elevator and make a wardrobe change.

"I'll handle it."

"You always do." He reached into the inside pocket of his jacket. He brought out an intricately designed tube of lipstick before handing it to me.

"Your purchase from Danika. She would have delivered it herself, but nausea got the best of her."

I took the container with the microchip at the bottom, our fingers brushing for the barest of seconds. A charge sparked between us as it always did when we touched.

"Sam, this won't happen again."

"You're the last person to lie to yourself. You know as well as I do that if we are alone in a room, there isn't a chance in hell it won't happen again."

I lifted my chin. "We are with different people."

"And yet, we cheated on them without a second thought." He stared into my eyes. "Now think on this. How long will it take for the Joshi prince to figure out the Queen of Diamonds likes to slum it raw and dirty with a New York City street rat over a prince with a palace?"

Before I could respond, he pushed me back and shut the door between us.

4

SAM

I ENTERED MY PENTHOUSE IN THE KING HOLDINGS BUILDING a little after one in the morning, wanting nothing more than a stiff drink. But I'd already had my two-drink max for any night. It was my hard-and-fast rule.

Maintain control at all times. A level head won every battle.

Alcohol, drugs, and addictive substances of any kind resulted in poor judgment.

Then what the fuck was I doing with Devani Patel? She had her hooks in me, and no matter how much I wanted to break free, I couldn't move on.

Throwing my jacket on an armchair, I entered the kitchen, filled a large glass of water, and chugged the contents.

Loosening my tie and unbuttoning my shirt, I moved to the floor-to-ceiling windows in the living room. The bright lights below hummed with the energy of life in New York City at night. Some were living an adventure, while others sat in a pit of despair.

Sometimes, it still surprised me how I'd ended up in this life. I'd gone from an orphan kid who'd fallen through the cracks of the foster care system to one of the wealthiest men in NYC.

I owed it all to Arin King. His no-bullshit methods taught me everything I needed to know and gave me the tools to play in a world that those born without a silver spoon could never join.

Bracing a hand against the glass, I rubbed the back of my neck, where I bore the marks of Devani's nails.

Devani Maya Patel.

The Queen of Diamonds, as the press and society had dubbed her. No one would find a silver spoon in her box. Instead, she'd eat with cutlery made of priceless jewels, diamonds, sapphires, and rubies.

She acted the part of cool, collected, bitchy-to-the-core socialite. Still, the real Devani cared and loved harder than anyone I'd ever known. Though she'd go to her grave denying it.

I couldn't help but shake my head. The woman was vicious when riled, especially when set on a cause or target.

She'd never hidden the fact she wanted to destroy the family who took her parents from her, but I'd never expected her to sell herself to Joshi and, in turn, to that fucker Shah.

Because it was well known, any place Arun Joshi moved, Ashok Shah was next to him. They'd created the image of perfect friends in their personal and business lives. Though I knew most of it was bullshit. They played up the happy bromance for public consumption.

Joshi had never gotten over losing his oldest son and beloved heir, Lukesh Joshi. The asshole Shah had tried to force Jayna to marry not once, but twice. As far as the world believed, Luke was very much alive and taking a leave of absence from the family business. However, he'd passed into the afterlife over a year ago and hopefully sat in a special place in hell for helping Shah plan and orchestrate the car crash that nearly killed Kir and then the mugging that had resulted in Jayna never being able to carry her own children.

The thought of anything happening to Devani at Joshi's or Shah's hands had a rage like nothing I could understand burning in the pit of my stomach.

Sooner or later, I'd have to accept she'd picked a different road.

I'd offered to give her the revenge she sought, and she'd laughed. The thought of depending on anyone else or letting them help her was a foreign concept for her. All the years of leading teams in Solon made her believe she was the one who solved all the problems. Sometimes things weren't so black and white.

Hell, she was Solon. All of those fuckers worked in the

gray. They broke every rule, bending them to fit a situation to reach their end goal.

Fuck. I sounded like a wimp with a broken heart. I had to get it together.

My reputation was at stake.

I was the King brother born without a heart, the one with ice frozen in my veins instead of blood. The man who never met a deal he couldn't bend in his favor or a card game he couldn't win.

If only I'd let the queen stay on her chessboard that long-ago night instead of taking that dare she'd thrown my way. Since then, we'd spent nearly three years pushing boundaries neither of us knew we had.

My cell rang in my pocket.

Pulling it out, I read the display and answered with, "Delivery made with minimal bloodshed."

"Too bad. A good stabbing always puts me in a good mood." The humor in Danika's voice had my lips curving. "Did she complain about the color again?"

What would Danika think if she knew her fashionista best friend never even glanced at the color of the lipstick in the tube hiding the microchip at the base?

"No complaints that I heard."

"I'm sure she'll send them my way with her next order." She quieted for a moment as if to gather her thoughts. "Sam?"

"Yeah."

"Did she look okay?"

"She's beautiful, Dani. Not a hair out of place."

Well, until I got my hands on her, but I kept that part to myself.

"You know what I mean. Devani's keeping something from me."

"She keeps things from everyone, even her own people. I highly doubt she tells you everything, best friend or not."

"We are the only people she lets in. Actually, I think you may know more about her than I do."

"I'm not part of the equation anymore, Dani. She made her choice."

"She doesn't love him. You have to know this."

"I've moved on."

"Have you? Disappearing from a gala to fuck someone doesn't mean you've moved on."

So, the family had noticed my absence.

"Weren't you on your way home with this morning, afternoon, all-day sickness? How would you know if I was there or not?"

"I'm Danika King. I have my ways."

"Dani, did you call to ask about the drop or something else?"

"Sam, you're my family. I can worry about you if I want."

I sighed. "I love you too, little sis."

"See, was that so hard?"

"Good night, Dani."

"Bye."

I hung up.

For being younger than me, she played the big-sister

role pretty much like an expert. The fact she'd called to check on me, knowing the drop would have left me raw, showed how well she understood me.

I was the King without feelings, but Danika saw through my bullshit. She'd built the same type of wall to survive the fucker, Shah. I could still remember how she held her head high, even when people commented about her cold persona time and time again.

Jayna's temperament leaned on the scale toward fire, where she would blow up and fight everyone who stood in her way. Danika tipped in the opposite direction, all ice, freezing out the world if it meant others left her alone to do what she wanted.

The one exception was Nik. He'd seen through her cool veil to the fiery woman underneath. From the time we ran the old neighborhood together, the two of them had intense chemistry. Once they reunited, their youthful love turned into something explosive.

Kir and Rey had the same deep connections with their wives, Jayna and Lilly.

Then there was me.

Only one woman had ever made me crave something more, a future outside the one Arin had molded me to take. Then she'd chosen the easier path, a life she claimed to despise with every fiber of her being. A life where she felt as if she had no choice but to sleep with a knife under her pillow.

The chime of the service elevator rang out, making me wish I'd thought to lock down access to my place.

If it was one of my brothers, they'd get a punch to the face for bothering me so late. Fuckers made it a sport of dropping in unannounced to see if I had anyone over.

Danika, Jayna, and Lilly usually sent a text before they came over. *Usually* being the operative word. If something riled them, they'd come into this place like a tsunami flooding inside.

The only other woman who'd ever crossed the threshold of this place was a Solon director who'd invited herself into my home. And to this day had never used the front door to visit me.

She'd utilized her vast array of resources to acquire the early nineteen-hundreds blueprints for this building and then followed the hidden crawl spaces into the service elevator shaft.

Nothing ever seemed to scare her. Not the possibility of getting stuck in a tight space, caught by the top-notch security team guarding the building, or detected by the state-of-the-art monitoring system Danika had installed along the perimeter and floor. Even the very real threat of my shooting her with the arsenal strategically hidden throughout each room in my apartment hadn't deterred her.

The slide of the elevator shaft said my guest had arrived, but the absence of footsteps meant it could only be one person: Rey's wife, my sister-in-law, Lilly. I viewed her as a Jane of all trades—spy, hacker, mob princess, and of course, former Solon agent. Although when I thought about it, I highly doubted she'd stopped aiding and abetting her former director altogether.

"Knock, knock," Lilly said in a British accent as she came into view.

She wore her dark brown hair piled into her signature messy bun atop her head and a loungewear set. Her stormy gray eyes swept the room, taking in everything from my attire to the level of the alcohol in the decanters at the bar.

Cop eyes, as I liked to call them, from my days on the streets.

"What can I do for you, Ms. Cora Hass?"

She shot me a scowl for using her now-defunct hacker name. A name so notorious it had placed her on the CIA and Interpol's most wanted list. And probably, at least eight other countries' most wanted lists, if I thought to look.

"You think you're so funny. Don't forget, if you piss me off, I can make leaving your ultra-tech-savvy home very difficult. Then how will the property raider Samir King move about all his billions on his chessboard?"

"I would never think of upsetting any of the King ladies. Each one is lethal."

My statement barely scratched the surface when describing Danika, Jayna, and Lilly. Each woman possessed knowledge and skills to boggle the mind, and when they combined their efforts, one better watch their back.

The fact any of my brothers could hold their own with their wives was a feat in itself.

Then again, Nik, Kir, and Rey needed women who

wouldn't put up with any of their bullshit. Street-hardened men required partners who accepted them but pushed back when necessary.

I moved to the stocked bar in the back of my living room, poured Lilly's preferred spirit, and then handed it to her before moving to the leather armchair near the windows.

"Is this late-night visit business or something else? Dani's already conducted her required sisterly check-in."

Lilly remained quiet for a few moments as she sat on the sofa across from me and then asked, "Is your relationship with Van over?"

Van, the operative name for the Director of Solon North America, Devani Maya Patel.

To Lilly, Devani was the director who risked her life at every turn to protect her agents. The leader who'd use any trick in the book to ensure the innocents had a chance to see another day. Hell, Devani had taken on the directors of another continent to save Lilly and Rey out of pure loyalty to Lilly.

"I was never in a relationship with anyone named Van."

"You know what I meant."

"What is it specifically you want to know?"

"Would you help her if she were in trouble?"

Something prickled at the back of my neck. "Want to elaborate on that question?"

"I just need a simple yes or no. Did Devani burn her bridge with you?"

"The queen is the most volatile piece on the chessboard.

Simple is the last word to use when describing Devani Patel."

"Would you rescue her if she needed it?"

I almost laughed at the thought of her calling for a rescue. "She would go down in a fiery inferno, taking anyone and everyone possible with her before asking for help."

Lilly held my gaze. Her gray eyes darkened as she studied me in the same way her mentor loved to analyze me.

"Would you come to her aid, even if she refused to ask for assistance or if she wanted you to join one of her schemes?"

I smirked. "Now that was the right question."

"And?"

"And what?"

Lilly threw her hands in the air. "I swear the two of you are fucking perfect for each other. I always feel like I'm going in circles with you. Maybe all of these years together had some of her company training rubbing off on you. Every one of us knows she broke your damn heart."

I kept my face emotionless, giving away none of the turmoil boiling inside me. Lilly read people like the back of her hand. I'd give her nothing to latch onto.

"How can anyone break something that doesn't exist? I'm the King with an empty space where my heart should reside, or don't you read the news articles?"

"Oh, for fuck's sake." Lilly jumped up and began to pace. "Could I get a little emotion, please?"

"Would you rather have me stalk her across two continents and blackmail her as Rey did to you?" I kept the ice in my tone, knowing I was being a complete dick but not giving a shit. "Or maybe I should angry fuck her in the women's locker room so loud that everyone in the gym knows I staked my claim on her."

"Well, it would be a change of pace over this shit," Lilly retorted, cocking a hand on her hip and not taking my crap. "At least tell me you said more than two words to Van when you made the drop for Dani at the gala."

I almost smirked. Danika and Lilly wouldn't know what to make of my discussion with Devani.

I could still feel her coming around my cock. I hadn't planned to fuck her in the dark, but going into the secret speakeasy room brought back memories of countless encounters in the back room of The Library.

"We said more than two words."

"At least that's something." She paused as her sharp gaze narrowed, zeroing in on my face. "What happened to your lip?"

Shit. I forgot about that.

"An altercation that isn't any of your business."

"Then I guess the scratches on the sides of your neck aren't either?" She lifted a well-defined brow with a smirk.

"Is there a point to this?"

Lilly shifted around the sofa in a smooth, soundless pivot only achieved by years as a Solon Agent.

"Of course, there is. And you've answered every one of my questions while trying to avoid answering them. Solon

101. I may have left the job, but the training is ingrained in every one of my cells. You're as sharp as they come, Sam King. Yet, you never spent years under the tutelage of the queen of manipulation, aka, the Queen of Diamonds."

Irritation coursed through me. Devani and her fucking people, even in my damn family.

"Let me repeat, what the fuck is the point of this conversation?"

"I just needed to know if we had to force a contingency strategy in the future. Devani's stubborn and will probably fight us the whole way."

"And you think I'm part of a backup plan?"

"No, Sam. You are the plan, and I won't even have to say a damn thing for it to go into action."

"You are as frustrating to be around as your former boss."

"Thank you. My current one is just as wickedly fabulous."

She worked for Danika in her art gallery as an appraiser and an underground equipment specialist, the illegal kind.

"That wasn't a compliment." I threw my head back onto the couch.

"Too bad, I took it as one. But Sam—" Lilly's voice grew soft, causing me to lift my head, "—you can't put women like us in any category. We are the way we are because of our experiences. Van more so than the rest of us. All she's ever known is the organization."

Fuck. First Danika, now Lilly.

"You don't have to give me any details. I'm positive I know more than you do."

Surprise flashed in her eyes. "Never thought anyone could get a single one of her secrets."

"Lilly, I'm exhausted. Get to the point of this mindfuck conversation so I can go to bed."

Lilly sighed. "Fine. Van put everything on the line for me. She brought me to the US and protected me, knowing it would start a war between her and the European Directors Council. I am going to do the same for her."

Devani had done precisely that. She'd taken on her rival council in Solon when Lilly had done the one thing a European agent of Lilly's caliber wasn't allowed to do, fall in love. Devani had manipulated and maneuvered people, assignments, and cases to have Lilly transferred to the US. She'd gone as far as having Rey, a CIA agent at the time, blackmail Lilly into working for him.

"Devani isn't stupid. She never goes into anything without knowing every detail. I'm sure she has every angle figured out, whatever she is doing."

I couldn't help but defend her. No matter how much she pissed me off, she calculated all outcomes for any possible scenario.

"Not this time. She's too fixated on getting results. She's not seeing all the signs and is putting herself in danger."

Everything inside me froze as the pieces of what Lilly hadn't said clicked into place.

"She's working an operation, using Joshi as her lead

into that circle." I focused on Lilly, but her face remained cool and void of expression.

Devani fucking broke us for Solon? No, this made no sense. She'd worked cases countless times without ending things between us.

Then I asked, "Since when does a director of any continent take on a lead role in any operation? Directors are too valuable. They aren't in the line of fire."

"I'm retired. The agency revoked my clearance a long time ago. I wouldn't have any knowledge of any active ongoings."

The fuck she wasn't aware.

I shook my head. "Looks like I'll have to go to the source to find my answer."

"Maybe you should. Third-party information tends to have details missing." She smiled and then moved to the area leading to the service elevator. "But keep it in the shadows. The queen is commanding a lot of attention now and has too many eyes on her."

"Have you ever seen us in the light of day?"

"No."

"Have you ever seen us together at all?"

"Not to my recollection."

"I know how to handle my business."

5

DEVANI

"IF THERE ARE NO MORE QUESTIONS ON THE UPCOMING VOTE, I propose we adjourn for the day," said Alana Tran.

Alana was one of my Solon field agents and the chief operations officer for Maya Ratna Holdings, the mineral conglomerate I'd inherited from my parents, Rishaan and Darshana.

I sat beside her, counting the seconds before I could escape this bullshit meeting with my uncles, Nishant, Naresh, and Hiren.

Every few weeks, they insisted the executives and board meet in the guise of an operations update as overseers of the inheritance my father left me. When in fact, they held only honorary positions since I'd controlled everything from the moment I'd turned eighteen.

I owned eighty-five percent of the company. This allowed me to place people in leadership positions I trusted and would keep my interests safe. Such as Alana and six others. In addition to knowing how to run an international mineral organization, they possessed skills I utilized for activities of an underground nature.

"I have one question."

I looked up from my papers to stare into my condescending Uncle Nishant's eyes. Whatever he wanted to ask, he meant to undermine my authority in this boardroom, as usual.

Fucker.

I'd dealt with the bullshit since I was eighteen and continued to face it at thirty-two.

When would he realize I possessed the ability to make chalk dust out of him without trying?

They'd thought sending me to boarding school would get rid of me and allow them to take over the legacy Papa had created from the inheritance my grandfather had given him. But that very institution gave me the resources to become the cunning bitch who sat before them today.

"If this is regarding the vote, you may ask it. Otherwise, let's wait until later." I would not let him derail me.

"My question is regarding the future standing of the company. Therefore, voting on acquisitions of mining operations may come into question."

The board members, excluding my uncles, shifted in their chairs as the tension in the room built.

It had been a long time since any explosion had

happened in one of our meetings. Always on the part of one of the three stooges. I'd learned to school my feelings into an emotionless mask.

"After your marriage to Joshi, what are your plans for this company? Be warned, Maya Ratna has been in our family for over two hundred years. We will not become a Joshi subsidiary without a fight."

Oh, he wanted to go there. Fine. We'd go there.

Bastard.

I never put any of our dirty family laundry out in front of the masses. I guarded my privacy. However, if it meant shutting these fuckers up, I'd happily give them a reality check.

"Is that so?"

"Yes," my other uncle, Naresh, said. "We will fight for what is ours."

"Yours?"

Dear Lord, these men were delusional.

I stood, setting my palms on the table and peering into each of my uncles' eyes.

"My time is very limited, so I'm going to clarify this once and for all." I kept my voice no-nonsense and emotionless. "And if any of you dare bring it up again, I will throw you off this board. Maya Ratna's boardroom is a place to discuss business, not petty family drama."

"Now, wait just a minute," Naresh interjected.

Ignoring him, I continued, "All three of you gave up your claim to Maya Ratna when you took the cash inheritance from Dada. The company was in trouble, so you decided to bail rather than work to fix things. Papa, on the other hand, took Dada's legacy and made it into the empire it became. You're lucky that Papa's love for you allowed him to forgive you, and then he gifted a five percent stake to each of you as my caretakers."

I smoothed my dress and strolled to the chairs behind my uncles. "Now to the topic of fighting me. I own the majority of this company, and you can do nothing about it. Papa's will stated any of his living children, male or female, inherited one hundred percent of his assets. Your archaic belief that a female cannot stand at the helm of this company will never hold up in any court of law."

I moved to the front of the room, where a giant screen showed the projected higher-than-expected profits for the quarter.

"Next, let's look at some facts. During the years when my three benefactors ran this fine organization in my stead, where they shunted me off to a boarding school in upper New York and managed the day-to-day operations —" I pointed to the years on the screen, "—market shares dwindled, and we lost much of the gains acquired during the time Papa revitalized the organization. Look at what happened when an inexperienced eighteen-year-old demanded to come aboard and take her place at the table."

"Yes, you are brilliant. This does not answer the question we posed to you."

I rolled my eyes. "Let me put it this way. I have not, will not, do not need you or any other man or organization to come to my rescue. I've handled things better than the three of you put together. Do you believe I would need Neil or his father's aid? Married or not, I've got things covered."

Having had enough of my daytime soap opera board meeting, I moved to the door.

"I believe this subject matter is closed. The next time anyone decides to interrogate me about my personal life, ask yourself, would you pose those questions to someone with a penis."

Pushing down the throbbing headache brewing at my temples, I exited the boardroom and made my way to the elevators.

As soon as I entered the cab, I dropped my head against the steel wall.

It wasn't even ten o'clock, and the day was a complete bust. Hopefully, something would come up to improve it.

Almost on cue, my smartwatch beeped with an incoming message.

Lifting my wrist, I read the display.

NOAH: *Up for a house party where we play a little game of hide-and-seek?*

Immediately, my mood perked up.

I slipped my encrypted phone out of my handbag and responded.

ME: *As long as I get to wear a fun catsuit and lay mousetraps.*

NOAH: *I wouldn't have it any other way.*

ME: *What kind of house should I expect to see? The Queen of Diamonds has very discerning tastes.*

NOAH: *This particular mouse lives in a very, very large, expensively gaudy and old house with lots of tight corners and spaces I'm positive the queen will enjoy.*

Ashok Shah.

ME: *Is the guest list curated? I don't want you tricking me and having any other mice showing up. I'm not particularly fond of his circle of friends.*

NOAH: *Goodness, aren't you a demanding diva? I promise you are safe from rodents.*

ME: *Then, count me in. Send me the detailed party invite.*

NOAH: *On its way. See you tonight.*

The elevator opened, and I strode out of Maya Ratna Tower with a smile and a spring in my step.

A nice B&E job with high-tech gadgets would definitely make up for the clusterfuck of this morning.

I fucking loved walking the line between criminal and hero. Morally gray was my jam.

"Go in three, two, one." Noah's voice called through my earpiece, exactly five minutes past midnight. "You have ninety minutes to run the gambit of the passageways. We need you to make sure all of the old access points are still clear after the renovations Shah made as a gift to his new bride."

I rolled my eyes.

"I know how to do my job. I trained your ass. Don't make me send you back to your pig farm in Colorado for insubordination. I'm the one in charge of this operation," I grumbled as I set my tracker to active, placed it at the opening of the hidden crawl space under the Shah Mansion, and then slid inside.

Shah's new wife, Amish, the Widow Noor, as I'd known her most of my life, fit all of the prerequisites for the exact type of society wife he sought. A woman who looked fifteen years younger than her age and knew how to carry herself in society. Most of all, she came with a sizable portfolio of her own.

Oh, and she was as conniving as Shah. They made the perfect match.

"I breed horses. I expect the Queen of Diamonds to know the difference between horses and pigs."

"Yeah, yeah. They're both animals who shit on the ground." I passed between two pillars with barely a foot and a half between them. "Whoever goes in here can't be much bigger than me, or they will become part of the structure."

"I still don't understand how you never think twice about these jobs."

I set up six more trackers designed to scan the area and give measurements of the sector to a central computer.

"Well, only a few are born in every generation with the ovaries to handle the tough situations."

I moved to the inner wall that I knew neared Shah's monstrosity of an office.

"Not all of us are the size of pixies."

I snorted. "Or can handle seeing bugs. Don't forget

these scary little passages have these creepy crawly things called insects living in them."

"Okay, children." Neil's voice came over my earpiece. "Let's play nice. Not to take Carter's side or anything, but you aren't normal, Van. You like playing in holes that have the potential of collapsing."

"As I said, you need ovaries to handle the hard jobs. Weren't you the one who spent three weeks in bed with allergies? I haven't taken a sick day except when one of you forced me to take one. And that was because I had three bullet wounds."

"I had malaria, Van. Not allergies." The annoyance in Neil's voice made my jab so satisfying.

"I had it too, but I didn't complain about it."

We'd been on the same assignment in the Congo and received a bad preventative vaccine batch. The whole team contracted the infection, requiring all of us to helicopter out and regroup. In a matter of a few days, I'd fully recovered and returned to duties.

It annoyed the hell out of Neil and Noah that I rarely, if ever, got sick. But then again, I dealt with a lot of other shit, so I'd take any positivity thrown my way.

"Hate to break up this banter between our superiors, but—" Tasha Lee broke into the conversation, "—we are on a timetable, and according to the infrared, it looks as if you're about to get company."

"Thank you for keeping us in line." I couldn't help but smile.

Neil and I had a reputation for staying on the hard-ass

side of things. Noah, not so much. Giving our team this not-so-professional side of us had probably shocked the hell out of them.

Almost as if on cue, the moment I crouched down to move through a low-lying area, the echo of voices reached my ears.

"Going silent," I whispered. "Shah's office is occupied."

Taking ginger steps, I positioned myself close to the area where, a hundred years ago, the owners had created an escape route, but Shah had sealed it up. Luckily, he hadn't completed the job perfectly, allowing me a tiny view into the room.

"We shouldn't be in here. If Sir finds out we are snooping, do you understand the consequences?" a male voice pleaded in Gujarati.

All of Shah's staff spoke his native Indian language. It was a requirement for employment, and he allowed no other language spoken in the house unless guests were in residence.

A female responded in the same language. *"I don't care anymore. Danika said we could come live at her home. Even Jayna said we could go to Miami and stay with her mother. I won't let that man lord over us anymore. How can you condone what is happening?"*

"Danika is pregnant. What if he does to her what he helped do to Jayna? We can't risk anything."

"They are grown women. Not the scared little girls who lived under this roof. They are the reason the bastard has behaved this

way for the last few years. He needed Jayna to fund his lifestyle. Now that he lost the election, he's desperate to save face."

"He has his faults but wouldn't go down the path you believe to rebuild his fortune."

"I can't believe those words came out of your mouth. Sir ordered the accident that nearly killed Kiran King. He helped orchestrate the stabbing that caused Jayna's miscarriage. That poor girl will never get to carry her own children because of him. And you were there when he paid off the truck driver who pulled out in front of the bus that killed over twenty people to keep Veda Kumari from meeting his parents."

A chill ran down my spine, and a lump formed deep in my throat. The elder Shahs had always known there was a child out there. Now it made sense why Sara Shah had worded her will the way she had. The eldest of her grandchildren, legitimate or not, would inherit the majority interest in Shah International. She'd left nothing to her son.

"Don't ever speak of any of that again." Fear laced the man's words. *"Our children's and grandchildren's lives depend on it."*

"I'm talking to you, stupid man. And if ghosts haunt this godforsaken place, I hope they take mercy on us hearing my words. And I hope they choke the life out of Sir, Arun Joshi, and those corrupt diamond Patel brothers. Let's add the other jerks to it too. They all deserve to die."

"What has come over you? Do you have any self-preservation left?"

"No. I know Sir is hiding the Circle's buyers list. I'm going to hand it over to Dani. She'll know what to do with it."

"You are making assumptions. There is no proof he's part of it."

"I can't believe I stayed married to you for so long. Thank God our children got their brains from me. As Jayna would say, grow a pair of lady balls or get out of the way."

"Your language is completely disrespectful."

"I'm a woman in my sixties. It's time I said what was on my mind. Now get out of my way so I can open that panel he thinks no one knows exists. Are all men this stupid? He has to realize the people who run his house know where everything is."

"Don't lump me with him."

"Oh, so now you agree he isn't some innocent?"

"Woman, stop putting words in my mouth. I never said he was innocent."

I would have laughed at the crazy banter between the couple if only I could wrap my mind around all they'd revealed.

A panel slid open near my face, and immediately I froze. Then came a shuffle of papers.

"Oh dear Lord, some of these records are over thirty-five years old. I don't understand what this means. Is this what he negotiated with Joshi? That poor child. Tell me that he isn't evil. All of these men are pure evil."

"Kala, we need to leave this room now. Put everything back." A panic lit his voice, telling me whatever he'd seen was worse than they expected.

Now I knew who the couple was. It was Kala, the Shah

family chef. And her husband was Nimesh, Shah's butler for the last twenty years.

"I'm so happy Dani and Jayna escaped this place. I have no doubt he would have forced them into this. He would have sold them to one of these criminals. That one, Skylar Anton. He was here only two days ago. His son—this is so horrible."

Now we had the name of the last member of the Circle —oil billionaire, Skylar Anton.

"Why won't you listen? Someone will find out we came in here."

"Give me your phone. I have to send this to Dani. She'll know who to contact. At least Dani can stop the next one."

"Are you crazy? Sir pays for this line. We can't risk him finding out we know."

"Then what are we going to do? I won't be able to live with myself knowing I stood by and let him or that group continue to do this. We were trapped before. We aren't anymore."

"We'll come back."

"Don't lie to me."

"I promise. The corruption is beyond anything I expected. I know who to contact."

"Who?"

"First, put everything back. Then, when we are in our quarters, I'll tell you."

She sighed, and a few seconds later, the panels closed. Then, the door clicked and the hardwood creaked, telling me the couple had left this wing of the house.

Who would have believed a last-minute recon job would turn into an information windfall?

For weeks, I'd endured dinner after dinner with endless conversations about Neil and me producing the next generation of Joshis. And all I'd needed to do was crawl through a tiny space meant for a child and eavesdrop.

In less than thirty minutes, I'd learned more information than I had in over a month, specifically that the jackpot to everything we needed to blow open this case sat snug in that cubby of Shah's. And of course, the name of the last elusive member of the Circle of Ten.

On the positive, or maybe not so positive, side, at least I wasn't the only one who despised my uncles.

I could still hear the hatred in Kala's voice as she said, *"those corrupt diamond Patel brothers."*

Maybe she knew about my uncles' involvement in my parents' and brother's deaths.

No, I couldn't hope. I'd put the idea of learning the truth away long ago.

It had broken my heart to hear the worry and fear in Kala's and Nimesh's voices. Whoever they planned to contact, that person better protect the couple, or they'd deal with me.

"Van." Noah's voice snapped me out of my thoughts. "Get moving. Forty-five minutes left on the clock."

"Tell me you got the conversation through my mic."

"It's recorded and already sent to translation."

"It's loaded. Send a copy of the conversation to Neil."

"Meaning?"

"It means there's a jackpot inside that panel compartment. I have to get back here without anyone being the wiser. However, in the meantime, I've got something you need to pick up."

"What's that?"

"Skylar Anton."

"I heard the international waters around the Maldives are very unpredictable and choppy. His super-yacht may run into trouble."

"Want to call in some assistance?"

"Already done."

"Two down and eight more to go."

6

SAM

FIVE DAYS.

Five fucking days since my conversation with Lilly, since I learned Devani ripped what we had to shreds for a fucking operation. I still couldn't wrap my mind around it.

It was time to get my shit together.

I tightened my grip on the steering wheel of my Bugatti Chiron. Whenever I felt the urge to push the limits of my car without landing myself in jail, I came to this private motorway. It belonged to a Formula One racing team owner who owed the King family a favor or two.

I'd call ahead, the raceway manager would clear the track, and I'd have a few hours to run laps as I cleared my head of all the shit.

Sometimes I came here for the fun of it too. What was

the point of having a garage full of state-of-the-art machinery and not pushing any of them to their limits?

My brothers ragged on me for my love of sports cars, saying I'd lost the streets by flaunting our wealth. Then I'd find a set of keys missing because one of the fuckers had borrowed a car.

Dicks.

I'd never forget the life I'd lived in the old neighborhood. I still had nightmares of being so cold, hungry, and desperate for a safe place to live that I'd nearly become a victim of a trafficking ring when I'd found myself at the steps of a shelter that wasn't.

I probably wouldn't be alive today if it hadn't been for Nik and Kir. Nik had literally grabbed me and thrown my eight-year-old ass onto Kir's bike before I could walk through the doors of that building.

They'd been kids themselves, only a few years older but smarter and a hell of a lot more street-hardened.

I'd seen them in the neighborhood from time to time but avoided them since they were bigger and intimidated me. The moment they saved me, I'd given them my unwavering loyalty. Then, less than three months later, Rey joined our crew, and the four of us became inseparable.

Whatever life tossed our way, we handled it together.

I used to wonder how we never ended up in juvie for the number of times we scammed and robbed stupid tourists who wanted to visit authentic New York City neighborhoods. Even on that fateful day our lives completely changed because of Arin King, we had all been together.

We'd been so fucking stupid. And I still couldn't believe Nik, Kir, and Rey went along with my dumbass plan to rob the asshole who walked around as if he owned the neighborhood.

I thought I'd planned every detail out, from the distractions and the bumps to the pickpocketing. I hadn't expected the trained eyes and skills of Arin's security or for Nik to trip as he made the swipe for Arin's wallet.

To say we thought we were dead that day was an understatement.

But instead of killing our asses as we well and truly deserved for being idiots of the highest caliber, Arin surprised the fuck out of us and took us in. He gave us a home. He turned us into the men we were today.

And he gave us plenty of shit when we were "dumbfucks," as he liked to put it.

When Arin adopted us, he'd investigated our pasts and learned every fucking detail about us. He'd never kept anything hidden, giving us the cold hard facts.

That was when I learned Nik, Kir, Rey, and I had ended up on the streets because of one specific incident. An incident I'd known was the result of my existence, even if I couldn't prove it. And the fact that Arin pulled me aside to tell me about what he'd discovered told me he believed the same thing.

I clenched my jaw and pressed my foot down on the gas pedal as I shifted gears.

I could still remember the conversation I had with Arin that night.

"I want him dead. We know he's behind it."

"I'm not disagreeing, but tell me this. How are you going to prove it?"

"I share his blood. That's proof enough."

"Use your head. That means nothing."

"He hid what he did to my mother and wanted her dead to keep his money."

"Again, what does that have to do with proof? You're acting like an idiot kid."

"I am a kid."

Arin sighed and shook his head. *"Okay, so you want this revenge. How do you expect to get onto his property, let alone through his security, to complete your deed?"*

"I'll manage it." I paced as tears streamed down my face.

"Sit down, boy. You're not even fifteen years old. You have more hormones than sense."

"I have a right to avenge my mother."

"You want revenge?"

"Yes."

"Then get smart. Raging and carrying on like a dumbass without sense isn't going to solve anything. That's not how this world works. Cold, hard ruthlessness is how you get fuckers like Shah to pay."

"Am I supposed to accept he murdered all of our families? How will I face Nik, Kir, and Rey, knowing I'm the reason their parents are dead?"

"Did you kill them?"

"It's because I exist."

"I thought you were the smart one of the group. Did I make a mistake? You're the product of two adults making adult decisions."

"How do I accept this?"

"Do as I say. Get smart. Control those emotions."

"But how do I face the guys?"

"We tell them the truth about the accident. A mechanical failure on a wet road caused the bus to crash. However, since you can't prove foul play, there is no point in adding to their pain."

"You want me to lie to them?"

"What are you lying about? This is all your mind making up possibilities of the reasons for the accident."

"You know the truth as much as I do."

"Listen carefully." Arin leaned forward. "Truth is very subjective. Those boys need facts. Your brothers don't need any more pain added to their shoulders based on some truth you feel. I will never deny Shah is your enemy. He threw you away, took your legacy."

"So you're saying with him dead, I can't take back everything he stole from me?"

"Exactly. Men like him need to suffer. Slowly, painfully, publicly."

"How?"

A smile touched Arin's lips. "Learn the world your enemy walks in. Become part of it. Play the game so well everyone forgets you weren't born into it or overlooks it. Then, when you slowly take over, no one realizes what happened."

"Why aren't you telling the others to do this?"

"Each of you has unique talents, and I plan to utilize all of them. Be honest. No matter how much we polish Nik and Kir, they will never lose the edge of the streets. And for what I need them to do, I don't want them to lose it."

"What about Rey? He's the one with the genius IQ."

"Oh, I've already put him into training. He'll have a similar curriculum as you, but his volatile temper makes him a better fit in other areas. You are the one who will represent the family. You'll clean up so nicely that the New York elite will fall all over themselves for a piece of your time."

"I swear I will kill Shah the first chance I get."

"Boy, you aren't killing anyone. Sit your ass down." Arin laughed. "You need to grow some hair on your chest and let your balls drop. But when you're ready, you'll have gone to the right schools, speak using the correct words, know the right people, and wheel and deal with the best of them."

"There has to be more to this than my revenge." I'd learned from the moment Arin took us in that he had a motive for everything. He'd lost his wife and children in a territory war, and taking us in had surprised us. At times, we couldn't figure out why us.

"I have three reasons. First—" Arin lifted a finger, "—I want the King name to become synonymous with power in New York, if not the world. In fifteen years, hopefully sooner, everyone will know of all four of you in some way. And two." He lifted a second digit. "The best revenge is to live well in the face of one's enemy. Let Ashok Shah see the son he threw away sitting as a king on a throne while he lingers below."

"And if I still want to kill him after I achieve your vision?"

"I'll hand you the weapon to do it. But I feel that once you check those emotions, you'll have more fun fucking with Shah's business prospects. Death is too easy. Hurt them where it counts. In the bank account."

"What's your third reason?"

"You're my son now. Family isn't always blood. You are my legacy. I will never throw you away. You are my child until my dying breath. Even beyond that."

His words had meant more to me than he'd ever know. Arin wasn't the affectionate kind of father, but his words impacted us.

The King brothers were his legacy.

And I'd taken his saying, *"Hurt them where it counts. In the bank account,"* as my mantra.

It made me a cold-hearted bastard with ice in my veins instead of blood. But, then again, those were facts.

I was a bastard.

The only person who'd gotten me to soften had the same reputation I did. Where I controlled my emotions to keep from killing someone, she felt so much that she buried it under an avalanche of ice to keep from breaking.

We'd shown each other parts no one else knew.

And then she'd fucking walked away.

The engine rev pierced through my rage, making me realize I pushed a speed dangerously close to something even I'd consider reckless. The last thing I needed was to spin out and crash. Easing up on the accelerator, I brought the sports car down to a more manageable pace.

I had to maintain the facade of the ultra-controlled

King brother. Sometimes, I would have loved nothing more than to let my emotions loose as Rey and Kir allowed themselves to do. There were only two places I'd had any freedom to let out the animal inside me.

The first was in the cage at the underground fight club Jayna and Kir owned. Knocking the shit out of someone while avoiding the same thing happening to me helped focus the aggression I locked away.

Usually, Rey and Kir stepped in as my go-to sparring partners. They understood my need for aggression release and wouldn't pull any punches. We were also similar in build and fought more on the mixed martial arts side of things. On the other hand, Nik preferred the heavyweight-boxing style of fighting and would clock my ass into next week.

I wanted to exert my rage, but I didn't have a death wish.

The second place I'd had the freedom to let out the animal inside me may never happen again.

I released a deep breath.

Every fucking thing led back to her.

Then again, what we had wasn't typical by anyone's standards. A secret committed relationship that had lasted nearly three years and pushed every fucking boundary possible.

Now she expected me to watch her parade around on another man's arm for God knew what reason. Because I sure as hell knew it wasn't just for a damn operation. Devani Patel always had an alternative motivation for every fucking thing.

What was so crucial for her to place herself in the middle of a chess match with the two biggest bastards in the Indo-American financial sector? Every fucker with a brain knew the bromance between Joshi and Shah was an act. They used each other for monetary advantage, usually with Shah at a disadvantage.

Hell, Shah had sold Jayna to Joshi's oldest son, Lukesh, as a way to pay off debts he'd incurred to build this empire.

Too bad, Lukesh never took heed of the Kings' golden rule.

Never threaten one of us. We won't think twice about calling in the right favor or personally getting our hands dirty. In that asshole's case, both had happened. He'd become fish food in the Atlantic when he decided to collect on Shah's deal.

Now, Joshi kept Shah on a tight leash, since, in his eyes, the amount due had increased tenfold. If I were him, I'd cut my losses and move on.

Then again, morons stuck together.

And Devani was right there in the mix of it with Joshi's other son, Neil.

Something about that one never sat right with me. He reminded me of someone, but I couldn't put my finger on it.

Then the way he watched things, very much like a cop.

But if Neil was one, how the fuck had he let his father and brother do the shit they had? Well, unless he was on the take.

No. Something about Neil reminded me of the way Rey carried himself. Rey's role in the CIA had helped the family and vice-versa.

I highly doubted another of Rey's types had ended up in the CIA. Rule followers rarely took people from our questionable backgrounds into their ranks, much less two from the same area.

As if Arin were smacking the back of my head, I figured it out and clenched my jaw.

Devani's words the night she ended things with me played in my head.

"For my plans to work, it requires a potential match with Joshi."

Neil was fucking Solon too. She hadn't left me for him. They were working on the operation together.

"Oh, Ms. Patel. Soon, we are going to have a nice long chat."

"I'M GLAD YOU AREN'T PLANNING TO SHOW UP ALONE. WHAT made you change your mind?" Jesika Rawal asked as she exited her limo upon arrival at the Altus House, one of the event spaces owned by her father.

I offered her my arm. "Let's say I have a few people to annoy."

"Oh, goodie. We have the same mission."

"Want to share the names on your list?"

"Absolutely not. It's a need to know." She shot me a

grin. "Besides, you are just as tight-lipped about the people you like to poke into a frenzy of rage."

"I'm pretty open about who I dislike."

"Members of New York City's elite establishment don't count. And you need to remember you're one of them."

"I'm an interloper who learned the right speech and behavior." As we passed security, I handed them my invitation, but as soon as they caught sight of Jesika, they handed the envelope back to me and stepped out of the way.

However, a few other team members began scrambling, and others began speaking into wrist mics.

"You fit better than I do, and I was born into it."

"I take it you forgot to let your family know you would be in attendance and bringing a guest."

"My sister knew, and now my parents do."

"So the grass isn't greener on the elitist side?" We stepped into the ballroom, and immediately a sweep of attention shifted in our direction.

Jesika's lips curved in that calm smile I'd seen Devani don so many times whenever she wanted to mask her emotions. "Didn't Jayna and Danika fill you in? It's sunshine and roses. And if you don't follow the establishment, the ladies and daughters with all the power make your life so easy. They talk about you to anyone who will listen and then point out every one of your flaws. Then, your parents will meticulously groom you and force you to attend all the parties to prove you are the perfect example of an upper-crust socialite."

The sarcasm in the description of her youth had me chuckling. She could definitely give Jayna a run for her money in the "just keeping it real" department.

"What could one of the most successful litigators in New York have done to fall from grace in her family's eyes?"

"You mean, besides, show up at an exclusive charity dinner with Samir King?"

"Exactly."

"Oh, so many things," she hummed. "Chief among them, I stood on the opposite side of the line they drew in the sand."

"So under the 'Miss Perfect, I always follow the establishment' guise is a rebel."

"Duh. You know about the outdoor sports I enjoy."

"Speaking of those sports, are you playing anytime soon?"

"I'm always playing. Everything else is a side gig."

"When did you start playing?"

"Is this curiosity, or do you want to join a team?"

"From what I heard, you have to start young. I doubt I qualify."

"We do start young, between seventeen and eighteen usually. I only know of one exception, much younger, but I'm sure there are others."

No. Only one exception ever—Devani. According to Devani, when the North American directors had learned her education started the day she turned thirteen, all hell broke loose. They viewed the actions of her trainer as grooming a child to become an assassin before they could make a conscious choice. However, Devani believed her trainer gave her a purpose and helped her survive her childhood.

Her mentor had also given her the skills to play on the shark-infested chessboard she'd have to navigate as the heiress to Maya Ratna Holdings.

"I believe your sports league president is unique in every way possible."

Devani came into view as if on cue, crossing the threshold of the ballroom on Neil Joshi's arm.

From the first moment I saw her, she'd had this aura. It was how she gave no fucks or couldn't have cared less whether anyone loved or hated her.

Though, feeling lay heavier on the latter side of the scale.

Jealous fuckers, all of them.

Growing up, I'd wonder what it would feel like to be the wealthiest person in a room, and then I'd gotten to know Devani. She rarely, if ever, trusted anyone and viewed the world with suspicion.

"Hot damn. Doesn't look anything like a league president tonight," Jesika said with a hum of admiration from my side. "She sure knows how to make an entrance."

"Queens always do."

I had no doubt she'd planned everything to command attention, to own the room. From the way she precisely applied her makeup to coordinate with the bold blue, body-hugging modern-styled lehenga choli she wore to how the priceless diamonds and sapphires covering her hair, neck, and arms reflected the light to give the correct impact.

She ignored everyone around her except Joshi, who seemed to keep a dialogue of some type going, which she responded to without changing her demeanor.

The fact they made a stunning couple had every instinct I'd spent years schooling down roiling and raging to burst free.

I shouldn't have expected it to be easier knowing this was an act. As long as she was on another man's arm, walking with him in public in the light of day, I'd feel this way.

Fuck, maybe I should have gone down to the cage for a sparring match with Kir or Rey. Kicking the shit out of them would calm me down enough to get me back to a manageable level.

All of a sudden, her dark gaze locked with mine.

The familiar energy I associated with her crackled between us.

Her eyes heated, and her lips parted for her to release a tiny breath, then she touched her tongue to her lips. Reminding me so much of that first time she'd walked into the poker club and challenged me to a game.

The night we'd gone from being one of the King brothers who bartered for favors with the Director of Solon North America to us, Sam and Devani.

My body responded as it always had when faced with her hunger and lust. Good thing my tux jacket covered the heavy bulge along the front of my pants. No other woman drew me the way she could with a glance.

I wanted to fuck her, possess her, own her.

Her poised expression faltered, and the arousal clouding her eyes faded and turned ice cold with anger when her focus shifted to Jesika at my side. However, within a millisecond, she reined her emotions back under control, returning her mask solidly in place.

Except for the clenching of her jaw, only someone who knew her body inside and out would notice.

Good to know this jealousy wasn't just one-sided. It would make things a hell of a lot easier when we had our discussion.

"That was interesting."

"Care to elaborate?"

"My position in the league is to observe. I catch everything, even when I wish I didn't."

"Your point?"

"Whatever just passed between the two of you, let me give you this warning."

"That is?"

"They don't call her the Queen of Diamonds for nothing. It will take more than luck or a prince with a billion in the bank to break that rock-hard shell."

"Good thing I'm not a prince but a King."

7

DEVANI

MY CAR PULLED UP OUTSIDE THE GLASS-AND-STEEL BUILDING where I lived.

Weeks of playing this role to perfection, of being the picture-perfect Queen of Diamonds with all its fakery, were taking their toll. Every inch of my body hurt from lack of proper sleep and exhaustion.

Relief washed over me, knowing I wouldn't have to constantly watch my back in the safety of my own place. Right now, all I wanted to do was shower, grab a bite to eat, and clear my mind with an extended meditation session before I slept.

Tonight was supposed to have been easy. I would listen, collect information, and report my findings.

However, Sam's appearance at the fundraiser had completely shot my concentration.

Why the fuck had he shown up? He wasn't even on the guest list.

No. I wouldn't lie to myself. My irrational reaction to Jesika had fucked with my ability to focus.

Releasing a deep breath, I pushed those thoughts back and looked up at the high-rise before me.

I owned every square inch of the building. Technically, Danika and I owned the property as part of a joint venture. However, since the world thought we were enemies, we kept that bit of news to ourselves, locked under a multitude of trusts and subsidiaries.

Danika understood my need to have a space where my uncles or their spawn had no access, where I felt like I could have a sense of peace from the world.

So with her help, we rigged this place with every high-tech gadget possible. I occupied the top two floors as my residence. And Danika and I used the rest for the headquarters of various businesses we owned, except for Maya Ratna Holdings.

I kept as much distance from that monster as possible.

It always surprised me how Danika and I meshed so well together. We were so different, from opposite backgrounds and upbringings.

She'd spent the beginning of her life in one of the poorest neighborhoods in NYC. That's where she'd first met Nik, Kir, Rey, and Sam. They were her family when she lost her mom, and her father worked like crazy to support them.

I couldn't say I knew what it was like to want anything. I'd grown up with the best of everything—food, clothes, toys, and definitely jewelry.

Maybe what drew us together was that soul-deep longing for connection—two orphaned girls who'd lived through the same heartache.

We met during her first year at Columbia when I'd approached her for an under-the-table job with Solon.

I still remembered the doe-eyed expression she'd given me when I'd cornered her between the rows of the library.

We'd both been eighteen but so different. Danika radiated innocence and a deep desire for escape, learning the ropes of her first year in university. On the other hand, having joined the organization at thirteen, I considered myself seasoned, anything but pure. I couldn't understand why anyone spent so much time in a library. The thought of going to college like any normal kid never crossed my mind.

To this day, it surprised people that I'd never sought a degree past high school. What I'd learned in Solon many would consider doctorate-level assassin training, but it was beyond unconventional.

Who was I kidding? I'd technically joined a cult as a child through a teacher at my boarding school. She trained me to become a walking hit woman with unlimited access to money and weapons. Then, when not actively on assignment, I spent hours upon hours learning how to run international corporations from other agents who ran businesses around the world.

Then again, I had no regrets.

Collette had saved me. If it wasn't for her no-bullshit stance or her support, I wouldn't have survived the loneliness or the fact I'd never fit in to the old-money, elitist school where I'd spent nearly every moment of my childhood after my parents died.

"The front security team is waiting for you outside. Will you need me again tonight?" Monti, my driver and bodyguard, asked.

"I plan to stay in. It's been a long time since I spent a night at home. I want standing orders that no one is allowed to come up. I don't care if a nuclear explosion is imminent."

He smirked at me through the rearview mirror and nodded before signaling the security crew outside my door to escort me inside.

Ten minutes later, I crossed the threshold into my two-story apartment. Just as I dropped my clutch onto my front entrance table and leaned down to slip off my shoes, my gaze landed on the only picture I had of my parents and brother with me.

A sense of loneliness washed over me. I'd gone from so much laughter, joy, and freedom to manipulation and having to watch every step I took.

What kind of person would I have been if they'd lived?

Would people still view me as cold and calculating?

Would I have had a family and children? Or would I

have rebelled and remained single as I was today at thirty-two?

No point in thinking about that. Those weren't the cards dealt in my direction.

With the hand I had to play, I'd made the choices for my future long ago. And babies and happily ever after weren't even part of the equation.

Maya Ratna Holdings and all of my assets would go into a trust for the three girls who were born into the new generation of my family. Women were rare in my family, and the girls belonged to the offspring of my asshole uncles, who I knew wouldn't leave a damn thing to their daughters based on how they treated them. They were all brilliant and deserved a chance to take the family legacy into the future.

At least, while I was at the helm, I could hire the girls as soon as they graduated school and put them in more than ornamental positions. Then they would have roles higher than their fathers and grandfathers.

Fuckers, all of them.

Shit. This lack of sleep was making me cranky as fuck.

First, a shower, followed by some mind-clearing meditation, then at least eight hours of uninterrupted sleep. And if anyone dared to bother me, I would knock them into next week.

Moving to the hallway leading to my bedroom, I stopped in front of a whimsical painting of an elephant and a little girl by a stream. I tapped my foot along a small pressure point between the wall and floor. A beam of light shot through the animal's eye, scanned my retina, and verified my identity. Then, an eighteen-inch thick, reinforced metal door popped open before sliding to the side.

After the room depressurized, I walked into my vault. The few people I'd allowed inside this space always shook their heads. It was a fifteen-foot by fifteen-foot armory and treasure box. Everything had its perfect spot and access criteria. Which meant the room would seal and gas would fill the space, knocking out the asshole who decided to touch my stuff without permission.

It was over-the-top and extra.

But then again, why not?

Slowly, I removed nearly ten pounds of diamonds and sapphires I'd strapped to my body tonight. I released a deep breath, feeling the weight of Devani Patel, Queen of Diamonds, lift from my shoulders.

Even the burden of Van, Solon agent and Director of Solon North America, no longer existed.

Now I was back to me, Devani, a woman with a lot of baggage who needed some chocolate and a good night's sleep.

After entering a code, I moved to the pistol display, removed my gun from the holster on my thigh, and left my vault to seal it.

Twenty minutes later, after a shower and a quick late-night snack of cheese, nuts, and chocolate, I made my way up the stairs to the top floor of the penthouse.

As soon as my feet hit the landing, I moved to the

oversized flat circular sofa in the bare space, crawled to the center, and sat. Then, using the remote on the cushion beside me, I turned off the overhead lights, casting the room into complete darkness, and opened the shades with another click of the controller.

Immediately, I was surrounded by three-sixty views of breathtaking New York City at night.

Inhaling deep, I took it all in. I loved this space. It was my refuge from the world. Where I could regroup and recharge.

I concentrated on the rise and fall of my chest while basking in the energy of the city below. The tension slowly eased from my muscles and mind with each exhalation.

I opened myself up to the thoughts of the past few days, weeks, and months. Some would take longer to understand, while others cleared faster.

First, I worked through all the daily issues I needed to process.

I had to stay the course, no matter how tedious the tasks became. I had to remember each useless dinner, gala, and event brought me closer to my goal. And every time I listened to another of Joshi's long-winded discussions, he gave me more and more information on the people in the Circle.

Arun Joshi wasn't the leader of the group, not anymore. Somewhere along the way, the power had shifted. And my gut said it all moved in the direction of Shah.

There was no reason for Joshi to keep up the charade of this bromance with Shah otherwise. Especially knowing

Shah was responsible for the loss of his favored son Luke and the continued control of the Circle of Ten into the next generation.

The fact Joshi had used his connections to eliminate a member of the Circle to make room for Luke without repercussion from the other members said Joshi wielded significant power. And for Shah to remain in the world of the living meant he held something substantial over Joshi's head.

I had to find a way back into the Shah mansion and that secret compartment. Better move that up on my priority list.

The next on my list was a hard one—time to work on releasing the anger and bitterness toward my uncles.

My losses remained the same. They couldn't take anything more from me. My position in life wouldn't change.

It was better to channel my energy toward the plans currently in motion.

Finally, I had to face that truth.

I bore the responsibility for my pain when I saw Sam with Jesika.

I'd walked away. Sam believed for another man. It was his right to move on, no matter the attraction we had for each other.

I couldn't sleep with him again. It was wrong. I couldn't compromise my case, my plans, everything I'd sacrificed.

I wouldn't hurt Jesika that way.

I continued to breathe deep, trying and failing to

release the turmoil of rioting emotions whirling inside my soul.

Controlling my inhalations, I returned my senses to the environment around me. From the sound of the air conditioner humming and the feel of my clothes to the tears I hadn't realized I'd shed.

At least I'd cleared two out of three big issues.

I fluttered my lids open and focused on a distant building.

Of course, I would zero in on the King Holdings building.

No matter how hard I tried to remove it, Sam's grip on me remained, but I couldn't repeat the actions of the other night. I had to stay away from him.

Cheating once was wrong enough. I refused to do it again.

The draw was too powerful, and as he'd said, any scenario with us in a room alone together would result in us fucking each other's brains out.

Being in the ballroom and dinner tonight felt like torture, especially with him seated only three tables away and directly in my line of sight.

My best bet was to avoid him at all costs, remove any possibility of interaction, pretend I felt nothing.

Tomorrow, I'd put someone on the task of learning the details of his daily schedule so I could implement my plan of self-preservation.

Now that I'd decided, it was time to power down. I

rolled my shoulders to loosen the muscles and then scooted to the sofa's edge.

Suddenly, I froze as I felt a familiar presence behind me.

"I love watching you meditate, especially your ability to concentrate and sort through all your worries. This one took a long fucking time. Could it be because you were puzzling through the fact that you broke us for a damn operation?"

8

SAM

I LEANED AGAINST ONE OF THE GLASS WALLS BEHIND DEVANI and smiled at having managed to sneak up on her.

In the rare occurrence it happened, I had to congratulate myself.

Her back stiffened, going ramrod straight. I had no doubt a jumble of profanity coursed through her mind, most of it directed at me.

It wasn't a lie when I'd said I loved to watch her meditate. She had this utter focus, this ability to tune out the world.

But it was something she only did in a place where she felt safe.

And no place was safer than her home.

No, that wasn't true.

She'd let down her guard when she knew I was there to watch her back. Meaning my place or on those rare occasions I'd ever managed to get her to meet me somewhere off the grid.

And even if she'd never admit it, the reason she hadn't felt my approach at all revolved around the fact that she knew I posed no danger to her. Her soul knew it, even if her mind warred with the thought.

"How the fuck did you get past the security Dani installed without having your balls fried off?"

"You're not the only one with skills or the ability to navigate hidden passageways."

I'd been with her long enough to expect her to have multiple pathways from her apartment without utilizing the front door or lobby exit. Over the years, I'd found every one of them. Also, I'd watched her input her eighteen-digit code for the security elevator enough times to memorize it.

Who the fuck had an eighteen-digit access code?

Devani, that's who.

"Liar. You came up the security elevator." She glared over her shoulder, her dark eyes shooting daggers in my direction. "You're such an asshole."

"And you're a manipulative bitch. I never complained about your quirks. So you shouldn't complain about mine." I moved toward her, making her sprint up and position herself in a defensive combat stance.

Even though I towered over her by a good foot and outweighed her by eighty pounds, I would never mistake her petite frame as anything but dangerous. She knew every trick in the book to disarm and disable an opponent.

"Sam, I'm not in the mood for any of your shit right now. I'm exhausted and have a busy day tomorrow, including an afternoon event. Go visit your girlfriend if you want to pick a fight."

"Highness, you're not the only one who's exhausted. And I don't give two shits about your event. Your social schedule is the least of my concerns. And for the record, Jesika is a friend, not my girlfriend. There is a huge distinction."

Her eyes darkened as she absorbed the last part of my statement, and the hum of energy charged between us.

I never believed I'd see the day anything could push Devani to a human emotion such as jealousy. If I survived tonight, I'd get to tell the tale.

"I'm going to bed. I'm not thinking clearly, and you're the last person I want to deal with."

"You're not going anywhere. Not until we have an in-depth discussion."

A crease formed between her brows. "The hell I'm not. Try and stop me."

"Is that a challenge?" I adjusted my stance, readying to block her access to the stairs.

"I don't need to challenge you. You came into my home. Get the fuck out." She stalked in the direction of the stairs, and just as she moved to pass me, I shifted to grab her wrist.

She ducked, punching me in the ribs and knocking the wind from my lungs.

"Fuck, that hurt."

"Good, it was meant to."

Before she could land a kick, I took hold of the foot she swept out, pulling her to the floor and then rolling on top of her.

"Get off me, you giant, moronic jerk." She pushed at my shoulders, unable to budge me.

As she struggled, I managed to pin both her legs down and then trap them under mine. I would not risk losing any one of my balls. And in her present state, she'd probably cut them off.

"No." I grabbed hold of her hands and then planted them above her head.

"Listen, King. I will fuck you up if you don't move."

I peered down at her flushed, enraged face.

She was so fucking beautiful. Angry or aroused, the storm in her dark brown irises made me want to fuck her senseless.

"We both know if you actually wanted to hurt me, you would have reached for one of the weapons you have hidden under that sofa or employed one of the Dim Mak pressure point attacks you taught Danika."

Resignation washed over her face. "What do you want from me, Sam? Nothing will change."

"The hell it won't."

"You think I'm going to shift my objective."

"I'd never make such a mistake. You are single-minded

when it comes to your assignments. The Director would never lead her team astray."

"Then why are you here?"

"To make it clear that you will never pull this shit, ever again."

"You believe you have any sort of power over me?"

"Oh, I know I do."

"Keep dreaming, King."

"Want me to prove you wrong, Patel?"

A crease formed between her brows, and her eyes heated with challenge and lust right before she quirked a brow. Immediately, my need to dominate her jumped into full force. Only this woman had ever brought out the caveman in me.

"You're too damn cocky for your own good."

I shifted my feet, making sure to keep her legs from escaping and her arms secured above her head.

Leaning over her, I said, "Are you conceding?"

"I never surrender." She lifted her chin as if she were the one in the position of advantage.

"Of course, you don't. A queen never admits defeat, even when she's pinned under her king."

"Don't, Sam." She jerked up with a surge of unexpected strength, freeing her hands, and covered my lips with her fingers. "Please, don't say things like that."

We stared into each other's eyes.

Brushing her fingers away, I asked, "What don't you want me to say? The truth? What do you think we've been doing for the last few years? The emotions don't go away with a snap of the fingers."

She swallowed, and before I realized what she was doing, she grabbed the front of my shirt and brought her mouth flush with mine.

Fisting her hair, I took control, deepening the kiss. A moan erupted from her lips as she clutched at the fabric in her fingers and then slid a palm up my shoulder and around my neck.

She always had the sweet taste of elderberry candy she favored mixed in with her delicious natural essence. It was like nothing else I'd ever encountered—haunting, mesmerizing, addictive.

"Sex won't make me forget why I came here," I murmured, nipping at her jaw and trailing down the sensitive skin along her neck.

"I'd never make that mistake." She arched, giving me better access. "You love your answers. Maybe I'm the one who wants to forget. More like needs to forget."

What the hell could she mean by that?

Before I could think further about her words, she flipped me onto my back, my arms captured by Devani's thighs and her sitting astride my waist.

"Who's under who now? Never forget, I've knocked fuckers bigger than you on their asses."

Damn. This woman made me so hard. Lethal and beautiful.

Her hair tumbled around her flushed face as she peered down at me through lust-glazed, almost black eyes.

That's when I noticed the dampness of tears on her shirt and the lingering sadness on her face.

Maybe this wasn't the right time for answers.

Staying relaxed under her body, I said, "Well, Highness. You have me in a very compromising position. What do you plan to do about it?"

"Let me think." She licked her lips and gave me a calculating smile.

Slowly, she pulled her tank over her head, revealing her full naked breasts, and then simultaneously ground her hips, back and forth, to rub her pussy along the length of my straining cock.

My eyes nearly rolled into the back of my head, and it took all of my control not to buck up against her.

She was a fucking tease.

She knew those minuscule boy shorts barely concealed the heat and slickness of her arousal.

Setting her palms on my chest, she leaned down and traced her tongue over the seam of my mouth. "I want to fuck you and then send you on your way."

The hell she was.

I narrowed my gaze. "Is that so?"

"Did I stutter?" She lifted a perfectly arched brow.

Without giving her any preamble to my next move, I sat up, capturing her wrists and then clasping them to the base of her lower back.

"Let's get this straight." I brought my face a hairsbreadth from hers. "I am not now nor ever have been someone you can dismiss."

"What are you, then?"

"An idiot for letting you set too many rules for far too long." I threaded the fingers of my free hand into her hair and jerked her head back. "That is all over. I'm setting this card game by my terms. And you want to know something?"

"What?" She all but growled out her response.

Pure outraged female radiated in waves from her.

"The house always wins." I leaned forward, biting her lower lip and giving her the edge of pain she enjoyed.

Her breath grew shallow. "You forget. I don't follow rules. My specialty is breaking them. I've made it an art form."

"I'm going to take that as a dare." I rubbed my jaw over her bare nipple and the swell of one breast.

"Take it whatever way you like. Right now, either get to fucking me or leave the way you came in."

I couldn't help but look up at her and shake my head. The woman never stopped giving orders.

"Are those my choices, Director Patel?"

I rolled us to the side, shifting my feet under me, and then lifted and carried her to the oversized meditation sofa in the center of the room. Once there, I unceremoniously dropped her in the middle.

"What the hell? You asshole." She scrambled onto her knees.

I unbuttoned my shirt and threw it on the floor, and then toed my shoes off. "Unrefined street kid from the blue-collar side of town, remember, Highness?

Unfortunately, I don't know the etiquette for handling a queen."

She clenched her jaw. "Unrefined, my ass. I'll show you unrefined."

I should have known better than to brace for her to come straight at me. Instead, she lunged from an off angle, wrapping her legs around my waist and digging her claws into my shoulders. Then, jerking her hips, she threw me off balance, and we landed sideways on the flat couch.

I panted, trying to catch my breath. "Fuck, woman."

Only she'd turn sex into a sparring match.

"Yes, fuck woman," she responded as she gasped in air. "I want it as you said three weeks ago. Don't make me beg, Sam."

As if her words unleashed the untamed animal inside me, I pushed up and caged her head with my arms. "And if you have bruises when you go to your fancy event tomorrow? How will the Queen of Diamonds explain things?"

"It's public knowledge that I'm a fifth dan in taekwondo and train regularly. I have bruises all the time."

I slid my hand over her throat and then squeezed. Immediately, her eyes dilated, and her breath grew shallow. "I doubt after a session with your black belt masters, your throat carries marks from fingers you begged to clamp down harder while you were on the cusp of orgasm."

"T...true." She squirmed, her hands grabbing hold of the belt loops of my jeans.

Shifting my body lower, I scraped my teeth over her

shoulder, causing goose bumps to prickle her skin. "I'm positive you never walked out of any match with bite marks on any part of your body."

I slid farther down, biting the swell of her perfect breast and making her cry out. "Oh, God. Nope. That's never happened."

I reached under the sofa cushion and pulled out a set of buttery-soft leather cuffs with a thin chain anchored underneath the couch. When she saw the restraint in my hand, Devani's breathing became even more erratic. She moved to a sitting position and offered me her hands so I could buckle the cuffs to her wrists.

After ensuring enough space in her bonds to allow movement but keep her from sliding out, I cupped her jaw and throat. "And, I'm absolutely positive none of them dared to shackle you to any surface and then proceeded to cause you to lose yourself to so much pleasure that your captor had to make sure you didn't rub your wrists raw."

"No, no one but you has done any of those things."

"Why is that, Highness?"

"You're the only person who gives me the freedom to let go. You're the only one I trust."

My fingers tightened for a microsecond. "Yet, you broke us. For what? An assignment? I know it's more than that. Tell me I'm wrong."

She kept quiet but held my stare. We'd promised never to lie to each other long ago, even if the truth was brutal. She'd broken up with me by telling me she was leaving me for Joshi because he fit into her specific plans.

Now I knew it was part of whatever her fucking assignment was, as well as some other motivation.

"I thought so." Releasing my hold on her face, I slid my palm down her neck and stopped in the valley of her lush breasts.

With the barest pressure, she understood and relaxed back, reaching her arms above her head. Standing, I glided my fingers down her abdomen over to the waistband of her shorts. Slowly I tugged them over her thighs, along her toned legs. Once I had her clothes discarded, I took hold of her ankles and set her feet into place on my knees.

I couldn't help but admire the beauty of the gorgeous woman stretched out like a sacrifice before me.

A slight flush tinged her soft golden skin as her tight, beaded nipples moved up and down with each breath, and desire darkened her eyes, turning them almost black. Her swollen labia glistened with her arousal and called for me to taste.

"Sam, stop staring at me and do something."

"You aren't in any position to give orders, Highness."

"You're punishing me."

"Making you wait is punishment?"

"You're so angry."

"Is that a question?" I slid her feet to the fabric-covered cushion.

"It's a statement of fact."

"Tell me, Highness. Why shouldn't I be? You tell me just enough information, so it's never a lie. But what you say isn't the complete or full truth."

"We promised never to lie."

I dropped my face until my nose just brushed hers. "You let me believe that you left me for another man."

"No. I said I couldn't see you anymore. And that my plans required a match with Joshi. I never gave you a reason why for either thing I said."

I bit her lower lip, making her cry out, and then pulled back just as she tried to close the distance between our mouths.

"You are truly the perfect agent, Highness. Manipulating and twisting words so you never lie but never reveal anything."

She shrugged. "It's who I am, what I am. We both started our training at thirteen, but you had a father in Arin. I had Solon. We are replicas of our teachers, especially me. I'm an agent, a creation of the best in the business."

"There is a life outside of the organization."

"The rules are still the same. Except in the real world, it's a solo game, and I have no one to depend on but myself."

"You have me."

She shook her head, her eyes clouding with tears for the briefest of moments. "I don't want to talk about this anymore. Nothing will change."

"You can't believe that."

"Please, Sam. I need you to make me forget. Just for tonight."

I studied her.

This beautiful woman had no defenses left. If I pushed too hard, she'd break, and the last thing I wanted was to hurt her.

I sighed and reached over her head, unbuckling her cuffs.

"What are you doing?"

"This isn't what you need right now."

"I know what I want."

"But it isn't what you need." I rubbed her wrists and hooked an arm under her knees and back, lifting her against my body.

"Where are you taking me?" She dropped her head against my bare chest.

"To bed." I descended the stairs, keeping Devani tucked tight against me as we walked toward her bedroom. "You need to sleep."

"Dammit, Sam, I'm not a child."

"Believe me, I know. I've fucked you in every way possible." I ignored her as she scowled up at me. "When was the last time you had a good night's sleep?"

"Last night. I slept a whole four hours at a five-star hotel."

On what planet was four hours a good night's sleep?

I set her on her feet, opened her bed, adjusted everything the way she liked, and helped her climb in. "I mean more than four hours straight without waking to train or work?"

"Does it really matter? I'm home. I'll sleep tonight."

We stared at each other as I took in the meaning behind her words.

She'd spent the last few weeks in the various Joshi properties around the country. She couldn't sleep if she was on the offensive. If she was working and had to stay on guard.

She offered me her hand.

Logic told me to put her to bed and leave. This vulnerable side of her wouldn't last long. Tomorrow, she'd go back to the armored woman with the impenetrable wall. I'd come to her for answers and then planned to make her come to me. I'd resolved not to chase her anymore.

Now here she was, needing me, making me feel. This woman had me so twisted that I wasn't sure what was up or down.

With a sigh, I shucked my clothes and moved in beside her. Almost immediately, she wrapped her body around mine as if it was the most natural thing to do.

Brushing the hair off her forehead, I said, "You don't have to be strong tonight. You can let your guard down. I'll keep you safe."

She snuggled into me and whispered, "Don't make me love you, Sam."

"Too late. You already do."

9

DEVANI

WITH A HEAVY SIGH, I WIPED THE SWEAT FROM MY BROW AND exited the alley outside my target's building. Navigating the crevices of the two-hundred-year-old building had taken longer than expected, which meant I'd get some shit from Tweedledum and Tweedledee. At least the equipment placement had gone without a hitch.

Pushing the communication link on my wrist piece, I said, "Data transfer in progress. I'm exhausted. Why did I agree to this after someone I won't name ditched me today? I could barely make it through the luncheon with the two Masters of the Universe patting themselves on the back with all their self-accolades on the many things they accomplished in life."

"To be fair, Neil bought you an entire red velvet cake

from that bakery you love to make up for the pain you suffered." Noah's voice came into the earpiece.

"Which doesn't help when a lady has to wear a skintight bodysuit and crawl through spaces in ancient buildings. I felt like a sardine in a can."

"No one told you to eat that much," Neil responded. "You could have saved it until you got home."

"As if any of the vultures on the team would have left a piece for me to take home."

Taking a set of stairs into a park, I turned a corner, stopped near a group of overgrown bushes, reached behind it, and pulled out a long jacket.

After shrugging it on and adjusting my hair to something more relaxed and in line with the pedestrians in the area, I made my way to where my security team waited.

As I approached my car, I caught sight of the King Holdings building and paused.

A lump formed in my throat, bringing forth all the emotions I'd tried so hard to ignore for most of the day. The impact hit me like a fist to the gut.

As if sensing my thoughts, Neil said, "Don't take this the wrong way."

"But?"

"This job took longer than when you had no schematics for a building and went in blind."

Of course, one of them had to say something.

"Was this a timed task?" I asked as I stared toward the renovated high-rise and thought of one specific man who lived there.

The reason behind my lack of concentration.

"More an observation than anything."

"Since my performance is faltering and I'm also on the verge of retirement, next time *you* go in. It only seems fair that my replacement works all the nooks and crannies of old buildings better than I do. Or how about letting our surveillance jockey take a go at it? I know how much he loves small spaces."

"What crawled up your ass tonight?" Noah muttered under his breath. "You need to call King and get laid. You're so much nicer when he's in the picture."

Ignoring him, I slid into my car and immediately closed my eyes.

Calling Sam was probably not the best idea considering what he'd said right before he slipped from my bed in the early-morning hours.

"New deck, new rules. All or nothing, Highness."

He'd set an ultimatum. One I'd expected a long time ago.

If only I could give him the answer he wanted. Which only meant we were well and truly over.

And hence the reason for my whirling thoughts all day long.

"Going radio silent on us?" Neil asked.

"No, just contemplating things." My gaze landed on the windows of the floor where Sam's penthouse lay.

"I was kidding about King." A tinge of worry laced Noah's words.

"Were you?"

"I'd rather you take someone up on a random screw than that."

"My last random screw was Sam. Are you sure that's what you want me to do?"

"Never mind. Ignore that I said anything. Keep being your bitchy self."

I couldn't help but laugh. "Noah, you'd make a terrible therapist."

"That's why I'm a horse rancher."

"Among other things," Neil added and then said, "Get some rest, Van. And use whatever means necessary to sort out what's bothering you. Things are about to get intense. We need you clear-headed and focused, Director."

I pulled the com-link from my ear as the line went dead.

Releasing a deep breath, I inclined my head to Monti in the car's rearview mirror, opened the door, and stepped back outside into the night.

Less than twenty minutes later, I worked through the passageways leading into Sam's penthouse. Ducking under an angled beam and cramped corner, I approached the access point.

A sense of apprehension filled me, making me wonder if he was home. Then I released a deep breath when I heard the smooth beat of a popular R&B artist humming through the wall.

Sliding the wall panel to the side, I slowly made my way inside the warmth of the hallway and into the living room.

Sam stood with his back to me. His gaze trained on

something outside the floor-to-ceiling windows giving views of the New York City skyline.

I'd found him exactly like this the first time I'd broken into this place. Lost in thought, a hint of loneliness, and an aura of a caged beast lurking under the surface.

My pulse jumped as it had then. But now, it went beyond lust.

Moving closer, a surge of some energy pulsed between us, and he tilted his head slightly to the side.

"I expected a visit."

"Is that right?"

"What I said to you must have eaten at you all day."

"Are you sure about that?"

"You don't like unfinished business, Highness."

"And?"

"It will have to wait. But, first, I have one word for you."

I swallowed as my skin prickled with awareness, and my blood surged with heat and arousal.

"And that is?"

"Strip."

I stared at his back.

"Sam—"

"I gave an order."

My breath caught, and my pussy clenched.

This wasn't why I'd come here. He knew it. He'd said as much.

Inside of pushing back at his demand, I shrugged out of my coat, letting it drop to the floor. Next, I bent down, unlaced my boots, and stepped out of each. Then, I grasped the zipper of my bodysuit tucked under my throat. Slowly, I pulled the metal down, letting the skintight material fall off and pool at my feet. Last, I removed my bra and my underwear.

When I stood completely naked, I waited.

He glanced over his shoulder.

"You are no longer in charge, Highness." He turned, walked to a couch, sat, then picked up a tumbler of a dark amber liquid in the same shade as his eyes.

He swirled the whiskey before taking a deep gulp.

"Now, I want you to crawl over here."

I clenched my jaw. It wasn't like Sam to be so cold, so removed.

"This is a punishment."

"How is this punishment? You've crawled for me before. And if I recall accurately, you loved it." He held my gaze. "The only difference is that you want my cock but plan to parade around town with another man."

"You know the truth. I'm not with Neil."

"You're not with me, either."

"I'm more with you than anyone else."

"Not good enough. Not anymore. No more waiting, Highness. I want it all. But that's something you won't give me."

I stared at him, not saying anything.

He had all of me, just not in the way he wanted.

"That's what I thought. Now crawl or get out."

I resisted the urge to flinch at the anger radiating from him.

So instead, I lifted my chin and asked, "Is this about getting one last fuck before we go our separate ways, Mr. King?"

"Why not? Fucking doesn't require an emotional connection. Think of this as a practice run for the future."

"You think I'll fuck you in the future?"

"Get us alone, and it's bound to happen. You can't get enough of my cock, and I sure as hell enjoy your cunt."

"Fucking without emotion. Is that what you believe we have?"

"That's what we will have."

Bullshit. He knew it as much as I did.

It had taken one night for the bond to form between us. Saying we had nothing wouldn't wash it away.

However, if he wanted to play it that way, I'd play his emotionless game.

I slid to the hardwood floor and moved in his direction on my hands and knees. With my eyes trained on his heated amber ones, I exaggerated the sway and shift of my hips, tempting him to look away.

He licked his lips, set his tumbler on the table next to him, and adjusted how he sat.

When I reached him, I set my palms on his slacks-covered thighs. Then slid my hand upward, his muscles bunching and flexing under my fingers.

His lips parted to release unsteady breaths, and a sense of satisfaction coursed through me. He couldn't be indifferent to me, no matter how hard he tried.

"You want me."

"My cock should tell you the truth of that." He took my hand and placed it over his hard, steely length. "I'm half ready to fuck you as soon as I sense your presence anywhere near me."

I held his lust-filled gaze, the pulsing deep inside my core growing to a painful ache.

Licking my lips, I cupped and stroked him through his pants, making sure to linger on his large, flared head.

"Take me out."

Without moving my eyes from his, I worked his button and zipper open and then reached inside his boxers and took his swollen, velvety hardness into my grasp.

God, I loved the feel of him.

I rose onto my knees, leaned forward, and stopped when my lips were a fraction away from the weeping crown.

I stared at him through my lashes. The urge to lick him, taste him called to me, but the coolness he displayed felt so wrong. As if he sliced at a piece of my heart.

This wasn't my Sam. My lover who made me lose control when no one knew I craved it. The only man who saw past the face I showed to the world.

"You know what to do. The longer I wait, the longer you wait."

Fine.

We'd see how long he could remain emotionless.

My mouth engulfed his bulbous length, taking him deep enough to hit the back of my throat.

"F—fuck. Devani," he gasped out and threaded his fingers into my hair.

I felt the vibration of my name as it rumbled down his body, giving me a greedy pleasure.

That's what I thought. Sam couldn't remain impassive while I deep-throated him.

Fisting him at the base, I worked him with my lips, tongue, and fingers, up and down. My cheeks hollowed and drew in rhythmic strokes.

His face no longer showed the emotionless mask but a play of desire and rage.

When his breathing grew unsteady and his grip on my head tightened to an almost excruciating level, I knew his hold on his control sat on the cusp of failing.

And for some reason, the bite of pain spurred my arousal to a fiery level. As if I'd burn alive without release.

Only this man could do this to me. Too bad fate and circumstance refused to let me have him.

I wanted to slide my fingers between my legs to relieve the ache building deep in my core. But, before I could follow through on my needs, his cock swelled, growing thicker and longer, and the first spasms of pre-ejaculate dripped onto my tongue.

Suddenly, Sam grabbed me by the waist, lifted me, positioned his cock, and slammed me down.

"Oh, God," I cried out as my back bowed, and stars exploded in the back of my eyes.

The delicious sting of his invasion seared through all my cells, melding with my overwhelming desire. This pain-filled pleasure only he understood. My pussy flexed around his throbbing erection, bathing it with a flood of my passion.

It was too much and not enough.

"Breathe, love." He pressed a hand to my chest as the other held my waist.

I followed his command, slowly filling my lungs with air, and I opened my lids.

Sam's flushed face came into view, all evidence of the angry lover evaporated for a moment. Only my dominant man whom I'd hurt. So many emotions and overwhelming pain stared at me, making my throat burn.

Just as fast, he locked everything down, returning to his previous cool, furious, aroused state.

He cupped my throat, drawing me forward. "Now ride me and take your pleasure."

Pressing my knees into the cushion of the plush sofa, I lifted a few inches, wincing from the lingering discomfort of his invasion, and then lowered.

"Go slow," he ordered, his fingers flexing along the column of my throat.

The intensity of his golden gaze sent a flutter deep into my core.

No matter how much he wanted to remain aloof, it wasn't possible with me. This thing between us ran too deep.

Resting my hands on his shoulders, I began a steady rhythm, rocking and undulating my hips.

That he remained fully clothed while I sat astride him

completely naked should have pissed me off. However, it drove my desire higher.

He knew I liked it this way. Not so civilized and definitely unrefined.

With each slide of his steely, hard length, a pool of need built deep in my belly, waiting, churning to overflow.

My nipples and breasts ached, and my clit throbbed.

Sam's fingers stroked along my throat in a teasing caress. God. I needed that push, that one little push to send me over.

"Ask me."

"Please, Sam. I'm desperate."

"That's begging. I didn't tell you to beg. I said, ask."

"Oh, God. I'm right there."

He grabbed hold of my hip, rolling and rubbing his pelvis against my clit, giving me the barest graze but not anything near what I needed to finish the deed.

"Ask."

"Sam, will you help me?"

"How do you want me to help you?"

"Take my control."

"And when I put marks on you?"

"I want them."

"Ask me to leave them on you."

"Will you please leave your marks on me?"

His hold on my neck tightened, and my pussy immediately spasmed. "I've already left my mark on you. You'll figure it out soon enough. But in the meantime, let's add some more."

He crushed his mouth to mine in a brutal, all-consuming kiss. He claimed me with passion and told me I no longer had any say in what happened the rest of the night.

He pounded up into my pussy, relentless, hard, unforgiving. It was exhilarating and exactly what I needed.

Untamed, dirty, nothing a girl from society should ever want.

"Sam, I'm there. I'm there. Harder, I need harder. I'll cover it up. Just do it."

His grip on my neck intensified, and my body and mind crashed over the cliff of bliss. My pussy clamped and contracted along Sam's hard length as he slammed over and over into me.

Only this man could do it to me. Give me this. Give me what I craved, what I needed. Tears streamed down my face as wave after wave of release flowed over me.

How could I go on in life knowing this existed and never having it again?

"Beautiful." His thumb brushed the dampness trailing along one cheek. "Now, it's my turn."

A shiver coursed through my body as I took in the raw hunger in Sam's eyes. He'd held back so he could give me what I needed. Now, he'd take what he wanted.

My barely waned orgasm woke, responding to his feral lust.

He pulled free of my body and stood, his heavily engorged, very erect cock a heavy presence between us.

Turning us, he set me on the couch and brought my legs around his shoulders.

"Sam," I gasped as he licked the length of my swollen labia.

"This is for me. If I could, I'd gorge on your pussy, day and night." His tongue pushed into me, parting my folds and teasing the sensitive tissues.

My hips lifted, and my body begged for more as he circled, flicked, and nipped my throbbing clit. Then, he thrust two fingers into my pussy, scissoring and pumping, while continuing to work me into a mindless frenzy.

"Sam. I can't breathe. I can't—"

My orgasm crashed over me in violent waves, forcing my limbs to shake and my body to writhe.

"That's the point. You need to know who owns your pleasure. Who controls it." He continued his vicious assault, drawing out my release with measured strokes of his tongue and fingers.

He slowly rose, cupped the back of my head, and kissed me. The taste of us engulfed my senses, something I'd grown addicted to over the last few years.

When he pulled back, his eyes flashed with a determination that had my heart aching.

He tugged me forward and repositioned me so my front faced the back of the couch. Then, climbing on behind me, he pushed me forward, gripped my bound wrists, and slid in with one hard thrust.

"Fuck," he called out. "I swear, there is nothing like sinking into your pussy."

I couldn't respond as he proceeded to pummel my body with hard, unyielding drives of his beautiful cock.

I had no leverage, no control. Sam fucked me with nothing but a carnal instinct for release, using my arms to yank me back into each of his deep plunges.

One of his thrusts hit that perfect tender spot inside me, and I cried out, "Oh, God. Do that again."

"Even bound and at my mercy, you give orders." The humor tingeing his response brought back the ache from moments earlier.

He repeated my desired movements while he shifted the hand holding my hip down between my folds and then strummed my clitoral nub in a maddening rhythm.

My pussy quivered and flexed. Sam's breath grew unsteady, and his grip became almost painful, the telltale signals he sat on the edge of his release.

"Come now," he ordered, pinching the sensitive nerves he teased between his fingers.

I exploded, pleasure and pain melded together, and then nothing but delicious ecstasy radiated out from my core. I gasped and arched, lost in euphoria as tremors shook my entire being.

Not a second later, Sam called out my name as his orgasm tore through him.

"DRINK THIS. YOU KNOW IT WORKS. SO DON'T COMPLAIN like you always do." Sam offered me a glass with some awful-tasting herb blend that had some miracle ability to soothe after one of our intense sex sessions.

I downed the contents, winced, then chugged the water next to the disgusting brew. "Thanks."

He lifted my chin, studying the skin on my neck.

We'd spent the last hour and a half in a sort of quiet, wait-and-see mode, staying silent for the most part. Then, after a quick shower, we'd fallen into our routine of a soak in his oversized tub, followed by him tending to areas where he expected bruises to appear.

Now here we were, at the meal portion of the evening.

It would all go downhill from here. It was inevitable.

Deciding to be the one to start the conversation, I asked, "Do you want the answers that you never got the other night?"

"No."

"What do you mean, no? You broke into my penthouse for them."

"I told you. I want all or nothing. I've finally accepted what we have. So it doesn't matter what you do. As long as you're fucking me, you aren't fucking anyone else. I don't share my lovers."

"What we have isn't cold like that."

"It is exactly like that. If I recall, you were the one who set the rules. Keep it casual. We fuck when the need calls to us, then keep going about our daily lives."

"It never was like that between us."

"You set the rules that first night, Devani. I've decided it's time to enforce them."

"I see."

He shook his head. "You haven't a clue. When you catch up, find me. Until then, we'll serve each other's sexual needs as our schedules fit."

"Sam, why are you doing this?"

"Because we're playing with my deck now, Highness. You want my time. You'll crawl for it. You'll beg for it, not the other way around. You're so used to having everyone bow to your command. It's time to see what it's like to be at a King's beck and call."

"Why are you being such a bastard?"

He gave me a cruel laugh. "Did you forget? I am one."

"You've never been cruel."

"Wrong. I've never been cruel to you. I gave you the best of me and ended up the fool. Those days are over."

"Sam, this isn't how I want it between us."

"Now you'll see what it feels like to have the precedent you set used on you."

I lifted my chin, letting everything inside me lock down so I wouldn't break in front of him. "If that's how you want it, fine. But sex is off the table. I won't beg for your time or for you to satisfy me."

"You'll beg. I guarantee it."

"I'm the Queen of Diamonds. I won't beg for any man."

"I'm not any man." He smirked. "I'm a King."

He glanced at his watch.

"I have an early meeting, and I know you made it very clear that sleepovers and such weren't part of the equation.

I'm sure you can see your way out the same way you came in."

Without a glance in my direction, he took the hallway to his bedroom, leaving me knowing there was no coming back from this.

Pushing back from the barstool, I took a deep breath and moved to the service elevator shaft. I opened the panel for the walkway to the back passages, stepped inside, and then moved in about twenty feet deep before I stopped, bracing my back against one of the brick walls.

I dropped my head back and closed my eyes.

I had to remember when this finished that I'd done it all for love.

A lump formed in my throat. Not once had I told Sam that I loved him.

Now, it would never happen.

Sliding to the floor, I wrapped my arms around my legs, and for the first time in a long time, I sobbed, letting all the pain I'd bottled up flow free.

10

SAM

I BRACED MY ARMS ON THE GRANITE COUNTER IN MY bathroom, resisting the urge to find Devani and apologize for being a heartless asshole. The shattered look in her eyes as each of my words landed would remain etched in my mind forever.

She'd braced for it, expected it.

Part of me wanted her to hurt, to feel the pain. Then there was the side of me who understood her baggage and her need to fix the world, to put everything she wanted second, including me.

I gripped the back of my neck.

Life was so much easier before I let myself feel.

Idiot.

I focused on my face in the mirror. I may have that

bastard's features, but so much of me was Veda Kumari. If only she hadn't passed down that ability to feel so fucking much that it took more energy than I wanted to pretend otherwise.

Leaning forward, I heard the trace echoes of crying.

That couldn't be right.

No. It was there.

Devani?

She never fucking cried. A tear or two, maybe. Never sobs.

I rushed out of my room and into the kitchen, finding it empty. Then, moving to the passageway near the service elevator, I opened the panel she used to sneak into my place. That's when I heard a hiccup followed by the faint shuffle of feet.

"Devani, come back."

I made it in no more than fifteen feet before the area narrowed too much to let someone my size pass.

Hell, it could barely fit a person with Devani's mass.

I never understood why she liked crawling into spaces like these. Using the light from my cellphone, I angled it in the direction she'd taken. In the dust on the floor were imprints of what I could assume were Devani's feet and body as she'd sat on the ground. And the wall she'd had her back against was the main one of my bathroom.

If I wasn't sure before, this confirmed what I'd started to suspect the other night at her place. I'd left my mark on the Queen of Diamonds in more ways than one.

A rush of anxiety, elation, nausea, plus a surge of emotions I couldn't describe passed over me.

How the fuck would we navigate this? I guessed it depended on her.

Turning back to the penthouse, I pulled out my phone and sent a message to the group chat with Danika and Jayna.

Time to consult with the sisters. My brothers had their uses, but this wasn't in their realm of expertise.

ME: *Hey, PITAs, I know I keep blowing you off. Want to meet up for a discussion?*

Almost immediately, Danika responded.

PITA1: *I doubt this has anything to do with what we want, so spill it.*

Not a second later, another text followed.

PITA2: *Sam, do you realize what time it is? Danika and I were watching a movie. This is the first weekend in three months I'm not at the club and can have a girl's night in.*

Shit. If Lilly was there, then she'd tell Rey. They had this damn no-secrets rule after they left their agencies. The last thing I wanted was for any of the brothers to know, especially when things were fucked. When it came to delicate situations, they were like bulls in a china shop.

ME: *Is Lilly with you?*

PITA2: *Why?*

ME: *And you wonder why I call you PITA. Answer the question, Jay.*

PITA2: *No, she's out with Rey.*

Thank God for small favors.

ME: *Do you have time in your movie-watching schedule to fit me in for a discussion tomorrow? Or I can just come up for breakfast since you two are having a slumber party.*

PITA1: *First, I want to know if I'm still labeled Pita1 on your phone. Then I can decide if I'm available. And what makes you think you have an invitation to breakfast?*

PITA2: *Same question but rephrasing it with Pita2.*

ME: *It's changed. I swear.*

Almost immediately, my phone buzzed with simultaneous messages.

PITA1/PITA2: *LIAR!*

ME: *What if I promise to let you change it to whatever you want? It can even be something like Danika the Great or Jayna the Incredible.*

PITA1: *I'd rather get Lilly to lock you into your penthouse with Devani and force you two to duke it out. You may survive the altercation with a few fingers and toes left. I'm not sure if you know this, but I learned my blade skills from her.*

Of course, I knew. Those blade skills resulted in Danika nearly gutting an asshole who decided to manhandle her during a poker night at The Library, which resulted in a major shutdown and cleanup event.

I took a deep breath. I might as well get their curiosity piqued.

ME: *Since you mentioned fingers and toes...that's the subject matter we need to discuss.*

I waited for a surge of texts to blast through my phone.

When no response came, I typed.

ME: *Hello. Where the fuck are you? I expected Jay to at least lose her shit a little or call me or something.*

The main elevator to my penthouse opened, and Danika and Jayna walked in. Both had their arms crossed, and their faces bore matching scowls. They wore pajamas and had their hair piled in some haphazard style atop their heads. The stark difference in their heights should have made them look like the odd pair, but they fit.

More sisters than cousins, as well as sisters-in-law.

I narrowed my eyes, taking in the designs on Jayna's top.

"Do those pajamas have dicks on them?"

"Yep." Jayna smiled and turned as if she was modeling. "All different colored ones. A rainbow of them."

"You and your strange sense of fashion."

That was when I took in Danika's set. Hers had something that looked like flowers but also labia, or maybe they were tongues. I frowned.

"He looks confused. Tell him what they are," Jayna coaxed Danika.

"Yes, help a dumb guy out."

"They're artistic flowers drawn to represent the female sexual organs. It was a present from Lilly. She has a set too."

Danika moved into my kitchen, opened the refrigerator, grabbed a fruit container, and then walked into my living room. "Come on. Family meeting time."

"It's one in the morning. I didn't expect the meeting now."

Jayna took a seat next to Danika. "You can't drop something like fingers and toes and expect our asses to stay in our beds."

"I'm still processing. So let's chalk it up to temporary insanity. Now, you two can return to your slumber party."

Neither of them budged, only glaring at me.

"Dani, you want to handle this, or should I?"

"Go right ahead." Danika popped a strawberry into her mouth. "You're the MMA fighter of our duo. Clock him a few times for me."

In the next second, Jayna jumped from her spot and grabbed my shirt. "If you knocked up some chick you are only banging to get over Devani, I swear to God, I will drop-kick your ass into next week."

Holy shit. She was serious about knocking my ass out.

"Calm down. It isn't like that. Give me some credit." I tugged at her clenched fists, trying to keep her from ripping my favorite T-shirt.

"Don't tell me to calm down. Do you remember when you decided to play big brother and threatened to kill Kir if he didn't fix things with me? I have the right to worry about you."

"Oh, for fuck's sake, Jay. The situations are completely different."

Kir had let Jayna believe he'd died after his near-fatal car accident orchestrated by Shah. Then, when he'd decided to get his head out of his ass, he wanted a second chance with Jayna. I'd ensured Kir understood that I'd break his face if he broke Jayna's heart again.

Kir was my brother in all things but blood, and we'd faced everything together, but Jayna was my blood and a sister I'd never had the chance to protect.

"First, tell me who's pregnant." She shook me with my shirt.

"It's Devani," Danika answered while she grabbed Jayna's arm, forcing her to release me, pulled her down to the couch, and tried to keep her fruit container from falling, all at the same time.

Jayna scowled at her. "You knew?"

"I suspected."

Like hell.

"What brought you to that conclusion?" I asked, giving her a "you are full of shit" glare.

She lifted a brow, returning my scowl. "I'm her best friend. I know things."

"That means nothing." Jayna pulled out a grape from the bowl Danika held and popped it into her mouth.

"I'm pretty sure I picked up on the same clues as our big brother."

"I highly doubt this. I see Devani naked. You don't."

"And you call me the PITA."

"No, I call you PITA1."

"Hold up. Hold up." Jayna's agitation brought a smile to my lips. "Someone needs to bring me into the loop, now."

"Devani is pregnant," I stated as fact.

Deep in my gut, I knew it was true. Too many things over the last few weeks brought me to this conclusion, and I had no doubt after tonight.

I'd noticed the subtle changes in her body, especially her fuller breasts. First from a distance in her gowns and then up close over the last two nights.

But it was the tears that had my mind churning with suspicion.

In the nearly three years we'd spent together, I'd seen her cry once, and that was when she'd recounted the story of her parents' and brother's deaths. And she'd only allowed a few tears to fall before she pulled the pain and heartache back into that box of hers.

Then in the last few days, I'd seen her lose her ability to hold it in. First, when I'd found her after meditating, then tonight during sex, and then her broken-down sobs in the passageway.

She wasn't a woman to ever let emotions push her. *Ever.*

Where I pretended to feel nothing, she slowed her ability to process emotions so much that nothing could penetrate her shields.

"Did she tell you, or is this a guess?" Jayna asked the question to both of us, but I knew she directed it at me.

"She hasn't even realized it yet."

"Then how can you even know for sure?"

"Let's say he's very observant when it comes to the director. They share a special kink that requires it." Danika lifted a defined brow.

I glared at Danika. "You really are a pain in the ass."

"That doesn't prove anything," Jayna insisted.

"Maybe." I shrugged. "However, in the next week, she'll figure out her trusty shot failed her."

I could almost see her blaming it on her cycle fucking with her or coming down with a bug when she never came down with an illness. But she'd know what really happened.

"For a man determined never to reproduce and pass on Shah's tainted genes, you sure are taking impending fatherhood like a champ." Jayna sat up, leaning forward. "Unless you aren't the father."

I narrowed my gaze. "The baby is mine."

The way we felt about each other, the connection we shared, wouldn't allow us to turn to anyone else.

"And?"

"And what?"

"You called us here for a reason, Sam. You need to come clean. Devani may be having a child you never wanted."

"It's not my decision."

"That's bullshit, and you know it." Danika smacked her hand on the arm of the couch. "Do you want this child or not?"

I hadn't realized how much I wanted a family, a future with Devani, until I'd held her last night.

"I won't force her to give me something she doesn't want."

The hardness on Danika's face evaporated, and something like pity replaced it. "You need to tell her how you feel."

"What changed your mind? You were so determined

never to have kids." Jayna stood, moved to my bar, poured a few fingers of scotch, and then brought it to me. "Drink. I know your clear-head rule, but you need to take the edge off and give us the whole story."

Sighing, I followed her order. As the potent liquid burned down my throat and took the expected effect on my senses, I wrapped my mind around the words I'd say.

"Both of you know how it started with us, or what we let you believe."

Danika and Jayna nodded in unison.

"We lied. We weren't the casual-fuck-when-the-itch-hit-us arrangement. Unconventional as it was, we were exclusive."

Jayna reached over and set a hand over mine. "Sam, you've never been good at hiding how you felt about her. You thawed for her."

"Well, if it makes you feel any better," Danika added, "to anyone who knew her, they saw how you affected her too. She's bitchy and snarky on a good day, but it went to another level when it came to you. In all the years I've known her, she's guarded her relationship with you beyond anything I've ever seen. You are the one subject even I can't touch."

I held Danika's gaze, knowing I had failed to hide the impact her words had on me.

Releasing a breath to settle my emotions, I continued my story. "At some point between the time you and Nik married and Rey and Lilly figured their shit out, I started believing there was a slight possibility for a future with Devani." I shook my head, running a hand over my face.

Jayna's fingers tightened over mine. "Devani became a priority, and you pushed your hatred for Papa to the back."

"I still hate the bastard, but the idea of giving him power over my future wasn't something I'd allow him to do anymore."

"Future meaning a family outside of our crew." Danika unconsciously rubbed the slight swell of her belly.

I nodded.

"Will you still want this baby, even if you two don't get back together?"

"Yes," I said without hesitation. "As Arin told me all those years ago, I was a result of adults making adult decisions. My child is the same. They are my legacy, Arin's legacy."

"Are you leaving the final decision on this to her, no matter the outcome?"

"Yes."

"And if she decides to keep the baby?"

"Then one of our issues is settled."

"And the other?"

"I can't do the same thing over and over again, then expect a different result."

"You love her."

I stared at Danika. "Was that a question?"

"I guess this means no more chasing the Queen of Diamonds?" Jayna hummed.

"I've played my hand. It's up to Devani now."

"Good. It's time my girl got a bit of her own medicine." Danika set the fruit container on the side table. "She's so used to bottling up her feelings that she thinks everyone has to play by her rules."

"Why do I get the feeling the two of you are enjoying the turmoil in my love life as if you're watching a show on your favorite streaming service?"

"Because we were in your shoes not so long ago. Payback's a bitch."

"I stand by my PITA setting in my phone," I muttered but narrowed my gaze as the two women passed glances as if sharing an unspoken message. "Just say it."

"Since you opened the floor up for discussion—" Jayna smirked.

"I have a feeling I'm going to regret this."

Danika folded her feet on the couch as if settling in for a debate. "Let's discuss the will."

I leaned back in my chair, knowing sleep wouldn't come for a while yet, and prepared for two of the most intelligent women I knew to give their reasons for taking everything from Shah.

"I'll listen, but I make no promises."

"At least that's more than we've gotten in years." Jayna stood as if she were about to present a case in court. However, the dick pajamas made it impossible to take her seriously.

"Well, let's start with legacies since you brought it up." Jayna glared at me and cocked a hand on her hip. "And stop laughing at my clothes. I have good points to make."

"Well, Jay. We do look kind of ridiculous with penises and vaginas on our PJs. Maybe we should take him to your place, and you can make breakfast. This way, food will distract him away from the multicolor dicks."

God, I loved these women. The world could fall apart, and somehow they'd find a way to make the shittiest situation better with their ridiculousness.

11

DEVANI

TWO WEEKS AFTER THE NIGHT WITH SAM, I MADE MY WAY
toward the kitchen of the Joshi mansion. It was a little
before six-thirty in the morning, and I hoped to avoid
everyone but the household staff preparing breakfast for
the multitude of guests in the house.

These dinners and house parties were getting on my
nerves. At least Neil's thirteen-year-old sister, Mia, was
here this weekend. Having Mia around had given me
someone interesting to chat with during the boring-as-hell
dinner last night.

A minimum of three cups of coffee were in order to
keep me from yawning all day long. Four hours of sleep
was just not enough to power me anymore. My body
seemed determined to wreak havoc on me lately.

Technically, I should blame Neil for my lack of rest. I'd spent the hours from midnight to two placing surveillance microchips in all the little nooks and crannies throughout the Joshi mega-mansion. Lucky me, the room Neil had assigned me for my stay had a hidden opening that led into the house's secret hallways.

The asshole could have taken care of this task long ago if he wasn't so paranoid about bugs and shit.

Now I was dealing with exhaustion, a backache from tossing and turning, and a major bout of queasiness for some weird reason.

Maybe I just needed to eat.

Man, even to myself, I sounded bitchy.

Yep, priority number one.

Coffee.

"Good morning," Mia said in a way-too-excited voice for this early in the morning, a few seconds before she engulfed me in a hug. "I'm so happy you're up."

"What are you doing up?"

"I couldn't sleep. I hate this house. It gives me the creeps." She glanced around the room. "It always feels like people are watching me."

Well, that wasn't something I expected anyone to say to me first thing in the morning. Especially not coming from Neil's sister. Which meant she had to suspect, if not know, some of the things her father had his hands in.

Neil kept details about his mother and sister very close to his chest. In such an extreme way, I took it to mean *don't ask*. It wouldn't have taken me long to learn the information if I wanted to dig, but I respected Neil too much to invade his privacy. He was my brother, as Danika was my sister, in all things but blood.

He let me keep my secrets, and I'd do the same for him. If he wanted me to know, he'd tell me. No matter what, we'd have each other's back.

I waited for one of the household staff who milled about the kitchen to interject, "Miss Joshi, it is just your overactive imagination. No one is watching you." But they all remained quiet while discreetly passing glances at one another.

As with the staff of every affluent family, they knew every sordid detail of their employers and were well-versed in keeping quiet. Some out of loyalty to the family they served, and others out of fear, as in the case of Shah's staff. I had a feeling the Joshi household ran things in a similar fashion.

"Maybe you can show me around later and point out where you think the eyes are," I suggested, releasing her from the hug. "But first, I need coffee."

I'd only had a handful of interactions with Mia, and each time, I noticed she only showed affection when she felt safe. She rarely hugged me, and it was only if her father or his friends weren't around.

The fact she felt anything but protected under her father's roof said Arun Joshi deserved every fucking thing we had planned for him

"They aren't ready to bring up breakfast yet. So I usually grab something from the pantry." Mia pointed to her bowl of cereal on the long farmhouse table in the back of the kitchen.

"I've got it. Everyone is used to my early-morning coffee runs."

Mia took her seat on the bench by her food and watched me as if she expected me to tell the staff to serve me.

If she only knew. I'd grown up in a boarding school where my teachers taught me all the rules of polite society but never once served us anything.

Then I'd gone straight into Solon life. No one gave two shits if I was a pauper or the notorious New York Queen of Diamonds. The only things that mattered were whether I completed my assignment and accomplished my set goals.

I could go from one day trekking through the middle of a jungle to sitting with a prince at a European banquet where the food most likely was poisoned. If I wanted to eat and ensure its safety, I had to get it myself.

Walking over to the staff breakfast nook, I filled a coffee cup, chugged down the contents, refilled my mug, and then took a spot next to Mia at the table.

Mia sat quietly for a few moments, pushing the contents in her bowl around with her spoon, then whispered, "When you marry Neil, don't live here. There are reasons why Mummy and I stay away."

All the hairs on the back of my neck stood up.

I leaned closer to her and responded in the same hushed tone. "What do you mean?"

"Things happen here." Her gaze shifted, and her back

straightened as a noise came from the hallway outside the kitchen, and then she lifted her spoon to her mouth.

Within the next ten seconds, Arun Joshi walked in. He came to an abrupt stop as he spotted me.

He wore slacks and a knit sweater, and his gray hair clung damp to his scalp, telling me he'd just showered. This casual side of him should have made him seem more approachable, except it only gave me the vibe this side was the actual predator, not the man who wore the suit.

"Why are you eating here? You should have called up, and they would serve you as is your station," Arun Joshi said in Gujarati.

I almost heard Danika's voice in my head, saying, "Station? What station, asshole? Gas Station, radio station. Fuck off with your station."

"I'm happy here. Eating here allows me to get to know the staff. And I have had the amazing company of your beautiful daughter."

"Ah yes, my daughter." Joshi studied Mia with so much disdain it made me want to take her into my arms and shelter her from his hatred.

What could a thirteen-year-old child have done to garner such a reaction from her father?

After he finished his angry perusal of his daughter, Joshi shook his head and said, *"Eating with servants is something you should get used to. You and your whore of a mother deserve nothing less."*

That had escalated quickly, and I'd barely taken a sip of my second cup of coffee.

Fuck.

Time to reevaluate my handling of this case. I'd heard too many similar things from my uncles in my youth.

Father or not, Joshi wouldn't treat his daughter like crap in my presence.

Sorry, Neil, I'm about to make toast out of Daddy Dearest.

Before I could give Joshi a piece of my mind, Mia jumped up from her seat, rage and hatred on full display for her father.

"You made her a whore. You sold her to your friends. You let them rape her."

"Shut up, little girl." Joshi stalked toward Mia.

"No, I will not shut up. You did this to us."

As Joshi reached the back of the kitchen, I pushed Mia behind me, leaped over the bench, and blocked her father's path.

"Have you lost your mind? What are you doing?" I shouted into Joshi's face.

"Stay out of this, Devani."

"You need to calm down and handle this rationally."

"I am handling a family matter. This girl lacks discipline."

He tried to shift around me, but I countered his movement, separating him from Mia.

"Discipline me, then. Let Devani see the type of family she is joining," Mia taunted from over my shoulder. *"Then maybe she will come to her senses and run as far away as possible."*

"I'm warning you, Mia."

Ignoring him, she continued. *"Tell her our big family secret. The one you go to such great lengths to hide."*

"Shut your mouth right now."

"Tell her you're sterile. Tell her how you prostituted your model wife in exchange for sons and lucrative business dealings. Tell her you aren't sure which of your asshole friends was Luke's father, and Neil's is someone you hate. Tell her the man who fathered me produced a girl, and you found a way to get rid of him."

Well, we just went from bad to a nuclear-level shitstorm.

I could really use some help here, Neil.

If only telepathy was a real thing.

"How dare you?" He tried to move around me, grasping at Mia's shoulder, but I shoved him in the chest with my forearm, sending him back three feet.

Surprise flashed on his cheeks.

Yeah, fucker. I so plan to teach your daughter the very same move to protect herself from jackasses like you.

"Don't you dare touch her," I warned him. *"She's a child."*

"No one insults me in my home. Least of all, a spoiled brat."

"Go ahead and hit me. It wouldn't be the first time." Mia shifted around me, daring Joshi to make good on his threats.

In the next second, his hand collided with her face. Then out of reflex, I punched him in the jaw, which brought blood spewing from his mouth.

Anger boiled inside me, and my fingers itched to tear this man to shreds.

But I couldn't, I wouldn't. Not now, anyway.

I locked down my rage and allowed my training to wash over me. Calm, collected, logical…mostly.

"You will not hit a child in my presence. You will not hit a child out of my presence." My voice no longer held any grace of the socialite, only the cool edge of the weapon created as a child. *"Listen very carefully. You attempt to touch her again, I will take great pleasure in breaking every one of your fingers."*

The room grew quiet as my threat pierced through the chaos of the altercation in the kitchen. The staff continued to work. However, they moved at a much more unassuming pace, as if afraid to make a sound.

I highly doubted anyone ever stood up to Arun Joshi, and if they had, they'd faced his wrath.

Here was the true Joshi. The one he showed outside of the public eye.

"How dare you threaten me?" Joshi redirected his rage from Mia to me, clenching his fists. *"Are you willing to ruin your relationship with Neil over a little girl you barely know?"*

As if hearing his name, Neil stepped into the room behind his oblivious father.

Anyone unfamiliar with his moods would believe the relaxed mask he wore conveyed disinterest or boredom. When in fact, it was the exact opposite. He held his temper in check by a thread.

The two people Neil cared about were his mother and sister.

I hoped Neil held it together long enough to resist killing his father in front of a roomful of people. It would completely compromise this case.

Hell, I'd already compromised this case by punching Joshi.

Shit.

We were fucked.

No. I'd think of something. I'd gotten out of more harrowing situations than this.

First, I had to get this douchebag handled.

Turning my nose up at Joshi, I said, *"Absolutely. She is a child. You are an adult behaving like a child. No, you are worse."*

"Have you looked into your family secrets? If any of those go public, my son will walk away without a second glance."

I couldn't help but laugh at this pathetic attempt to intimidate me.

"Big deal. My family sucks. Do what you have to, spread whatever you want about them." I leaned forward, getting in his face. *"I don't care. I'm the Queen of Diamonds. I know my value. You need me to hold your position in society. I know it, and so do you. I'm the prize all of you assholes want in your treasure chest. Too bad no one can own me. I'm fucking priceless."*

"Neil won't stand for this type of behavior."

"You really are going to beat this dead horse. Go ahead and believe what you want." I turned, taking Mia's hand. *"Mia and I will have some bonding time away from here."*

The way she grasped my fingers and the utter sadness in her eyes made me want to pull her into my arms.

Mia and I stepped around Joshi, and I purposely kept myself between him and his daughter.

As I passed him, he said, *"Neil is my son. He will choose me over you, any day. Family loyalty is everything to us."*

My gaze flickered to Neil, who moved in our direction. His arms opened, and Mia immediately released my hand and ran toward him.

"Are you so sure about that, Papa?" Neil asked as he wrapped his sister in a tight hug, and she buried her face in his chest. *"How will you get this heir from me if I don't have my chosen bride?"*

Without looking in Neil's direction, Joshi answered, *"There are many other candidates to replace her."*

"She isn't replaceable. She isn't a commodity."

Neil kissed the top of Mia's head and then gestured for her to leave the room. She nodded, glancing at me, and then rushed away. I had the urge to follow her, but I knew Neil needed me more at this moment.

From the beginning, our personal agendas ran side-by-side with the objectives of the case. Until now, I never truly understood the depth of Neil's hatred for his father. His motivation never centered around Joshi's corruption or the destruction of the company but on Neil's existence and his mother's pain.

It gave me one more reason to take these fuckers down.

Joshi for Neil.

Shah for Sam.

Sam.

A lump formed in my throat. No matter how hard I tried to push thoughts of him away, they lingered in the back of my mind. Maybe one day, he'd forgive me for what I'd done to us.

"Don't let your weakness for your mother cloud the way the world works." Joshi's raised voice returned my attention to the continued exchange between father and son. *"Your brother understood his duty. You will do yours."*

Neil came to stand beside me, drawing a glare from Joshi.

"Luke is dead. His duty, as you put it, made him stupid and cost him his life. I am far from stupid. And I know my duty, and it's to my mother and sister, not to you."

"You are weak. I should never have claimed you. You are no son of mine."

"Too bad. I'm all you have left. Luke isn't here to carry on your legacy. And you'll never pass anything on to the daughter I kept you from forcing my mother to abort."

A rage like nothing I'd ever felt radiated out from Neil. His breathing remained calm. However, the microscopic flex of his fingers gave away his readiness to reach for the weapon he kept holstered at his side.

The next words from his father would mean life or death. I couldn't let him take the fall for this.

Fuck. Fuck. Fuck.

I scanned the room. Six people.

They all looked as if they were ready to run but were too afraid to make a move.

Option one, kill everyone, call the cleanup crew, and make everything disappear.

Definitely not the best idea and not the way I worked.

Option two, kill Joshi, extract and relocate the kitchen staff, clean up the scene, and pretend ignorance.

Promising, but it would require a logistical nightmare.

Option three, let the bastard live and wing it.

I hated this part of my job.

I'd protect Neil, no matter the cost. But my gut said everyone in this room wished for Joshi's death. Which meant that option two was probably the best bet.

Only a few seconds had passed since Neil had made his statement, and I prayed I wouldn't have to act. I'd rather have Joshi's blood on my hands than on Neil's. He shouldn't carry the weight of killing his father.

"Why would I want a child she conceived by whoring herself to get a dime of my money?"

No such luck.

Before Neil could move, I kicked Joshi's feet out from under him, dropping him onto his back. Pivoting, I pressed the heel of my foot against his windpipe as I drew the gun I had tucked into the back of my pants and pointed it against his head.

The utter shock and horror and Joshi's face gave me a cold satisfaction.

Fucker still kept underestimating me.

"Give me the go-ahead, and I'll do it for you. You don't need this on your hands." I stared straight into Joshi's eyes, understanding finally dawning that I had no problems pulling the trigger.

"No, I want him to live. I've activated phase two of our plan.

And then when we finish this, I want him to see me give everything he has to the daughter he hates so damn much."

"I control this company," Joshi croaked out. *"You can't force me to do anything."*

Phase two. About fucking time.

Neil had called in our interrogation team. It also meant he wanted his scary side to come out to play.

"This is where you are wrong. Neil and I have skills beyond anything you could ever imagine. Something more on the spectrum of deadly." To prevent Joshi from speaking, I increased the pressure on his throat, causing a slight wheeze from him, and then continued. *"I'm no longer the Queen of Diamonds, and he's not the Joshi prince. And honestly, playing those roles was getting exhausting."*

I lifted my foot from Joshi's neck, and he coughed and sputtered blood.

He pushed himself to sit and glared at me but remained on the floor.

"Do you have any idea what you have done? The people in this room just witnessed you assault me."

As if on cue, a tingle shot down my spine, and I immediately knew Noah and our team had arrived.

They would gather the staff in the kitchen and relocate them to different lives with different positions.

Solon targeted and killed for a reason. We rarely allowed the innocent to become collateral damage.

"I doubt your staff hasn't thought of knocking you on your ass a time or a million since they started working for you. I only followed through."

A thought crossed my mind. How could the team have gotten here so fast? Neil could have only sent the message a few seconds ago.

The microchips.

Fine. I guessed the lack of sleep was worth it.

The team more than likely mobilized the second the argument with Mia started. I was never the type to stand by while anyone bullied a child.

Yep, I'd better prepare myself for a Noah Carter lecture on controlling my temper and kick-happy foot.

Confusion flashed on Joshi's face.

Still not understanding the dynamics of what was happening, he focused on Neil. *"Are you going to stand there playing her lapdog? I can't believe I raised such a pathetic son."*

"To answer your question, yes. As she is the ranking officer on this operation, I take orders from her. And for the record, you took no part in raising me. You didn't even provide the sperm for me."

Joshi attempted to stand, but I shoved him down with my foot. *"Thank you for becoming the man we needed you to be this morning."*

"You manipulated me into the altercation with my daughter."

I glanced at Neil, asking without words if he was ready. The slight twitch at the corner of his lips gave me all the confirmation I needed to end this back-and-forth.

"I would love to take credit for everything that transpired, but you made all of it happen on your own. Now, sir, you are about to meet someone no one would ever deem weak. Once he finishes, I'll get to play. Welcome to our world."

I stepped back as Neil leaned down, grabbed Joshi by his shirt, and hauled him up.

"Hello, Papa. I'm known as the Extractor. My specialty is working with combative informants. I believe you qualify. You are now my puppet. What you know, I will know. And if you even think about turning on me, I will make you pay for every single time you let someone hurt my mother while I was too young to protect her."

12

DEVANI

"THAT DRESS DOESN'T LOOK GALA-APPROPRIATE," NEIL SAID
as he stepped into the archway between my primary
bedroom and bathroom suite.

I glanced at him through the reflection in the mirror
above my vanity. "Another opportunity came up that I
couldn't refuse."

An opportunity to capture a European member of the
Circle who'd decided to visit the United States for an early
morning meeting with an associate. I wanted this heavy
hitter out of the country and tucked away in a nice cell
before sunrise.

I needed Shah agitated and suspicious of everyone
around him. And by taking out the broker who negotiated
all of the Circle's international deals and the person Shah

planned to enjoy breakfast with tomorrow morning, I'd accomplish my goal.

I expected Neil to eat my head later for keeping him in the dark. However, in my defense, I'd waited a full week after the incident and interrogation in which Joshi essentially became our walking, talking puppet.

And considering what I'd discovered while I snooped last night, I had to act the moment I heard the rumor of our perp boarding his flight.

But then again, if I'd told anyone I'd planned to sneak into the Shah Mansion again, they would have lost their shit. For weeks, my gut had been screaming at me to learn what Shah was keeping hidden away in that compartment.

Never in my life could I have guessed the rabbit hole ran so deep.

Now I knew that Shah kept records of everything. From his involvement with Veda Kumari and his constant updates on Sam's whereabouts, to the history of the Circle of Ten, the deals, especially every single person's contribution, and most of all, every member's dirty laundry, including his own.

I'd learned everything Mia had said that morning in the kitchen was true. Joshi had used his wife as a bargaining chip for deals, and there were five possibilities for Luke's father.

Then, there was Mia's biological father, the man Joshi had eliminated to make space for his son Lukesh to join the Circle: Kasim Simran.

He had been a Bollywood superstar who'd transitioned

into media mogul and died tragically, as far as the world knew, in an unexpected avalanche during an adventure vacation in Nepal.

Shah had collected names, dates, banking transactions, and even phone records of everyone involved in his death. The people involved in this scheme ran the gambit of political heavyweights around the world to real estate tycoons.

It was Shah's insurance policy to maintain his place in the world and the reason Arun Joshi kept up the charade of friendship when he hated Shah so damn much.

"What aren't you telling me?" Neil moved closer, taking a seat on the dressing sofa in the center of my bathroom.

"I never tell you everything. You should know this by now."

"You went to Shah's house last night after I told you to wait." His tone remained neutral, but irritation sat right under the surface.

We'd worked together too often for him to hide it, and he knew me too well to believe I wouldn't make an attempt on the house when I knew this was the last night Shah would be away on business.

"As of the last time I checked, I'm still lead. I don't take orders from you."

"Did you think of your safety, or is that something you don't give two shits about anymore?"

I never ran operations without proper monitoring, and he damn well knew it.

"Fuck off, Joshi." I narrowed my gaze. "I have to finish

getting ready. I'll share the details of my Shah Mansion snooping at a time and place of my choosing."

Ignoring my irritation, he asked, "So it's that bad?"

He had no idea.

Interrogating Arun Joshi, though satisfying to Neil, turned out to be mostly a waste of time. Outside of gaining his cooperation to do as we told him to do or suffer the consequences, Joshi had divulged nothing outside of anything we'd already discovered.

When the Circle had formed, Arun Joshi had commanded the most power and ran the group. As the wealthiest of the members, he'd financed everyone's projects. His price came in the form of DNA. He'd gone as far as hand-selecting which members out of the Circle of Ten would father his children.

This drive to pick the right bloodline had brought about the legacy program, an underground kidnapping and breeding ring. They provided heirs when a wealthy couple couldn't conceive the natural way. The women kidnapped weren't just random, but those picked for pedigree and background.

One day the women would be living their lives, then the next, they'd disappear.

My visit to Shah's hidey hole had revealed more than I could have ever expected, including a secret Neil would never want to see the light of day.

This had to be the foundation of why he hated his father so much and drove him to such drastic lengths to protect his mother and sister.

It could also explain Neil's reaction weeks ago at the ball when Shah mentioned not having a son. I'd seen the rage of murder in Neil's eyes, not only toward Shah but in Joshi's direction as well.

I could only imagine how it would feel to discover something like this about my own birth. Whatever the details, my heart ached for Neil and Mia. Maybe their mother had told them, or they had discovered it on their own. This type of reality was devastating all around.

Shah had kept records of every purchaser in the legacy program, every child conceived, and every woman whose life they destroyed. This included Arun Joshi and Shah's part in assisting him in achieving his goal of having another son.

Shah kept the information as if he reminisced in a personal diary to enjoy reading later. He'd written graphic details about everything, from how he'd forced Smita Joshi to conceive Neil to names and associations of the people he'd hired to kidnap Sam after his mother's death.

A kidnapping that never happened because Nik and Kir kept Sam and saved him.

"Yeah, it's that bad," I answered, my earlier annoyance with Neil completely gone and now replaced with a need to avenge him. "Tonight's not the night for the briefing."

"I'll let it drop for now."

"As if you had a choice." Reaching into my makeup drawer, I selected the perfect shade of lipstick, applied the color, pursed my lips, and returned the tube to its spot.

"You're seriously going to bail? On the night we're supposed to announce our engagement?"

"Abso-fucking-lutely. Though I do have to say, you look quite edible. Well, if I was into the runway, polished vibe."

He wore a custom-made white and black tuxedo and had his hair slicked back in a way only he could pull off. I called his look "rebel tycoon." Neil found my label less than amusing. In his opinion, cover models had titles like that, not spy agency directors.

"I'm very familiar with the fact that your tastes run to the underground, edgy type, even if they come in a three-piece suit." Neil gave a dramatic sigh. "As a director, you know this isn't how you're supposed to run things. You can't change plans at the last minute due to personal reasons."

My stomach clenched, and a wave of nausea coursed through me with the idea of wearing a ring given to me by anyone other than— Nope, not going there.

I checked my makeup one last time before walking into my closet for the shoes to go with my gown for the night.

"As a director, I can alter course as I see fit."

"It's because of King, isn't it?"

I glared at Neil through the open door. "There is nothing between him and me. That's over."

Since that night in the penthouse, all communication and interaction had stopped. He wanted something from me I couldn't give. Distance was the best solution.

"You agreed that, after the old man sang his uninformative song, the engagement was the most logical next step." Neil adjusted his pose on the sofa to keep me in his line of sight. "The sooner we announce our marriage plans, the sooner Shah throws us the party and his close friends from overseas gather for us to apprehend."

Not saying anything, I slid my feet into my stilettos.

"Talk to me. I'm one of the few people who understand complicated relationships. My better half took an assignment on a different continent because I fucked up."

"I don't have time for this. I have a job tonight."

"If I show up without you, it will cause problems. The news outlets are reporting about it."

"I can't, Neil."

"Why? Give me the reason, and I won't ask again," he pressed, propping his forearms on his knees and holding my gaze. "Or is it that you haven't even admitted it to yourself?"

I tightened my lips to keep from spilling my thoughts—too many things stirred inside me. Not only had my snooping revealed so many secrets, but it also revealed Sam wasn't Sara Shah's oldest grandchild and heir to her fortune. It was Neil.

Sam and Neil were brothers, half-brothers. No way in hell would I consider a pretend engagement with Neil.

It all felt like a Greek tragedy, but we were all Indian.

"I know the truth, Devani."

Instead of responding, I gave Neil a blank stare.

"It's okay to admit how you feel about King."

Oh. He meant he knew the truth about Sam.

Taking a deep breath, I said, "There is only one person's

ring I'd ever consider wearing, and the possibility of that is nonexistent."

"Why?"

"Because what I am and what I plan to do makes it impossible."

"That's bullshit."

"No, you have no clue what I'm talking about."

"Oh. I fucking do."

"What do you think it's about?"

"You plan to eliminate Shah. You plan to give his children and his niece back everything he took from them." Neil smiled. "We have similar goals, Devani. The only difference is that I'm doing it for my sister, not the man I love or my girlfriends."

Well, he had me there. Except now I'd added Neil to my list of people I was doing it for.

I moved to the sofa and sat opposite him. "How long have you known?"

"I confirmed it the night you met with your contact at the ball. Or should I say, your alternative contact?" I lifted my gaze, and he gave me a smirk. "Like you, I notice everything. Wardrobe changes in the middle of balls are extreme even for the Queen of Diamonds."

Since he'd never commented on my new attire, I'd assumed he'd chalked it up to my eccentric personality.

"I really hate you sometimes. Finish what gave me away."

"It was the look you gave Shah during dinner when he spoke about the future of his company and his wish to have a child with his new wife since grandchildren weren't in his future. I'd only seen you direct that cold, emotionless interest at someone you planned to target."

"As one of the Circle of Ten, he *is* a target."

"Cut the crap. I know someone on a personal hit list when I see it. Maybe it was the fact that King was also directly in your sight. You radiated this energy that screamed, given a chance, you'd have taken care of Shah in front of the entire ballroom and laughed."

"Are you going to tell me personal vendettas have no place in our business?"

"If I were a rule follower and speaking as the future Director of Solon North America, I'd say yes. The current director should know better and lead by example."

"But?"

"But. As someone working with my own demons and one of your closest friends, I'm all for clearing the world of trash like Shah."

A wave of guilt punched me in the core of my stomach.

What would he say when he learned that I knew all about his demons?

Pushing down my unease, I said, "I guess we understand each other."

"An engagement would make your end goal easier, if not much faster."

"When have I taken the easy path to anything?"

He sat up and then shook his head as he looked down at himself. "I wasted a good tux for nothing."

"You could skip the ball too."

"Is that right? And what exactly should I do with my time?"

"How about a flight to London? You can visit someone in the middle of a recon assignment at the parliament building."

I glanced at the antique clock on the counter behind Neil. Of all the people who needed a break, it was the man in front of me.

"You can take my jet, and a new team will start rotation by the time you land. That will give you forty-eight hours of uninterrupted personal time before your return flight."

"Director, are you telling me to abandon my duties for the weekend to get laid?"

"I wouldn't dare. I'm just looking out for the well-being of my subordinates. We all need a day or two to recharge."

"Are you going to do the same?"

I thought about the night ahead and hummed, "Actually, I'm going to have an absolute blast this evening. Someone sent me an exclusive invite to a poker night."

"Meaning you're going to The Library. Who is the contact?"

"Marianna Sonnita." I couldn't help but smile as I thought about her.

The fiery-tempered Italian knew how to have a good time. She ran the Sonnita Vineyards in Tuscany, which meant she led the Sonnita crime family. And just because she wasn't busy enough, she kept her hands full as a senior intelligence officer in Italian Interpol.

Tonight, we would play some cards, share some laughs,

and target the first of three European-based Circle of Ten fuckers. If all went according to plan, she'd have him on a flight to Rome by the early morning hours without incident.

"Do you remember the last time you two got together? We had to call a cleanup team to clear the damage from the beatdown you gave the perp."

Oops. I forgot about that.

I hoped things went according to plan.

I shrugged and said, "I wasn't going to let him jump us. He dealt with the consequences."

"Can I assume your King isn't the one in the house tonight?"

"I don't have a King." The quick way I responded to that statement revealed way too much.

When Marianna suggested The Library for the location to tag our suspect, I'd gone out of my way to ensure Sam wasn't the brother scheduled to oversee the club this week. The last thing I wanted was to have him screwing with my concentration, especially after that last night we'd had together.

Sam made me weak. Distance was the best thing for me. Then I'd finish my plan and move on with my life.

"Which of the brothers is on duty tonight?"

"Kir, obviously."

I'd recruited Kiran King as a liaison for Solon over a decade ago. Since then, we'd worked in trading favors here and there.

All the Kings were aware of our association but never

the depth of our business dealings. Kir aided in a gambit of ways, from introduction to the right members of various political organizations to brokering deals with high-level members of the underworld.

"Good. He knows your triggers and will handle things if they go south."

"Thanks for the vote of confidence."

"I'm being realistic. Two women with the same personality type and a history of volatile behavior. What could go wrong?"

"Go get on your plane and let me handle my business."

"Remember—" Neil's chiding tone had me lifting a brow, "—when I get back, you'll tell me all the details about your snooping adventure. You're keeping something from me on purpose. All I need you to do is confirm what I suspect you've found."

I ENTERED THE LIBRARY, FEELING THE WEIGHT OF THE attention of numerous eyes on me. They were those few members of New York's elite lucky enough to garner an invitation from the King brothers to enter their underground poker club. These few individuals had passed a strict level of scrutiny, from their financial and personal interests to every dirty little secret they kept. Most owed the Kings a favor in one way or another.

They also understood the rules of the club. Never speak of who one met or what transpired within the walls of the building. If anything leaked, the person committing the infraction suffered dire consequences. The Kings doled out punishments not by their hands but through those who owed favors.

Occasionally, they got their hands dirty, and those situations required major cleanup.

Everyone knew the brothers kept their word, and the people they called their own were protected and cared for like family.

No one fucked with them.

Therefore, the loyalty they harbored remained solid as ever.

As I passed through the body scanners, I nodded to the club's general manager, Amir.

His black eyes sparkled. His mouth quirked at the corner in a knowing way that said he damn well knew I had things strapped to my body.

His electronics and metal detectors were no match for what I packed. Jewelry could hide more than anyone would believe, as could shoes, purses, and hair accessories. Plus, the type of equipment I used never came up on any scanner.

This was a dance we'd played for years, and out of respect for each other's intelligence, we never pretended to be anything other than what we were.

Predators.

We'd run across each other in his former life as an antiquities dealer specializing in high-tech weapons. I'd hired him for projects requiring an untraceable touch.

However, once Kir had brought him into the fold of King Holdings, our association shifted to polite acknowledgments with no further business dealings.

He would have done well in Solon if not for his need for stability, family, and a solid future. Things that weren't guaranteed until complete retirement from the organization. And even then, it was questionable because of our high-risk lifestyle.

"Have my guests arrived?"

"Yes. Some are mingling among other attendants, and others are at your table. We will inform them you are on premises and ready for play."

As soon as he spoke, three attendants for the club left the holding area to follow through on Amir's words.

"Thank you. Would you also ask Mr. King to visit me once he arrives?"

He studied me for a second. "So we're clear, you're referring to Kir. Am I correct?"

I couldn't fault him for the question. The number of private games he'd coordinated for Sam and me over the years were too numerous to count.

Those days were long gone.

No more liaisons in clubs or penthouses or spots around the world.

I wouldn't lie to myself and think we wouldn't fuck each other's brains out if given a chance. Our attraction would remain intense and visceral.

But in the end, it would be sex, nothing more.

Pushing down my riot of emotions and keeping my face

devoid of emotion, I answered, "That is who I'm expecting since he is the brother on the schedule."

He nodded and stepped to the side as one of his team members approached. "Caso will show you to your table."

A few minutes later, I approached the impeccably dressed men and women at my table. They ranged in age from early twenties to mid-sixties. All garnered a net worth of at least one hundred million dollars and straddled the worlds of legitimate society and the syndicate.

I'd helped them all out of a jam or two in the past. Except for one blue-eyed brunette, who scanned me from head to toe as I neared the empty seat across from her.

She preferred to create situations others fell inside and then churn the pot.

"Ahh, there she is. Signorina Patel, we are ready to play. Yes?" Marianna Sonnita asked in a cultured Italian accent, giving a quick glance to the man who would sit to my left.

Of course, she'd placed the target next to me. The woman had at least eight inches on me and six bodyguards milling the room's periphery. They could grab the idiot if he made a run for it when we set things in motion.

Something in my gut screamed we had a runner.

If it turned into a cleanup situation as it had when the dick had tried to manhandle Danika, Kir would never let me hear the end of it.

In that case, the idiot shouldn't have tried to blackmail Danika into sleeping with him to keep quiet about her activities at the club. An angry woman with a sharp blade could cause a lot of damage.

"Absolutely, Signora Sonnita."

"I hope you are ready for a challenge. We have some tough players at the table tonight." She lifted her champagne glass, and the table laughed.

Oh hell, we had a volatile one.

Maybe I should have gotten engaged instead of coming here.

13

SAM

AROUND MIDNIGHT, MY CAR PULLED UP ALONG THE
alleyway adjacent to the building housing The Library.
According to the rumor mill, Joshi planned to announce
Devani's engagement to Neil Joshi tonight at a fundraiser I
would have attended as a King family representative. But
the last thing I could do was watch another man's ring sit
on her finger, even if it was all a ruse.

"Good evening, Mr. King." Amir, the club manager,
opened the door and greeted me. "We weren't expecting
you tonight."

"I decided to take Kir's shift tonight." Stepping out of
the car, I adjusted my suit jacket and lifted my face, taking
in the scent of baked goods wafting through the air.

Above the poker club sat its namesake bookstore and

cafe, The Library. Though it posed as a cover for our enterprise, my brothers and I ran the business as a proper independent bookstore. An up-and-coming chef from our old neighborhood managed the cafe, and a local retired teacher led the store staff. This was a local SoHo hangout, where people felt relaxed eating, chatting, and reading.

I glanced at one of my security, and he inclined his head. Then, he headed toward the cafe to grab the drink orders for our team, including a double espresso for me.

I moved into the hallway leading into the club.

"What are the updates for tonight?"

"Packed house, with more than our usual share of high rollers."

"Good thing I'm here and not Kir. He hates the meet-and-greet shit."

Out of all the King brothers, Kir was shy by nature and happened to be the one who hated anything to put him in the spotlight. So, of course, he was the best looking out of all of us. Even with the scars left from the car crash, he'd kept his pretty-boy baby face. And, of course, being the shy one meant he'd married Jayna. Her exhibitionist tendencies tended to make me want to gouge my eyes out.

No brother ever wanted to walk in on his baby sister doing anything sexual.

"That may be a problem. One of our guests specifically requested a meeting with your brother."

"They'll get over it. I can handle anything Kir can. Who's the high roller?"

Amir hesitated, making me frown in his direction.

"Spit it out."

"The Queen of Diamonds."

Everything froze inside me.

"What's she doing here?"

"She is holding court. It was an arrangement with your brother. A favor for a favor."

I clenched my teeth. "What kind of favor?"

"I don't ask questions, sir. I carry out details."

I stalked to the alcove where I could watch the proceedings in the gaming room without anyone noticing me. The room buzzed with energy as millions loomed in play at the center of each table. Excitement, anticipation, fear, regret, and elation coursed all around, and the level of each depended on the cards each person held in their hands.

The thrill of the unknown, the risk, the adrenaline rush, or all of it drove at something inside each of them.

I understood the exhilaration. Winning over one's opponents at the table and in life felt incredible.

Around the time I'd turned twenty-five, a reporter with an axe to grind against Arin and me published an article with a headline saying, "Arin King's Ruthless Heir: What Does a Gang Kid Know About Wall Street?"

When I'd come to Arin, pissed to holy hell, he'd laughed and ignored everything included in the article but the ruthless heir part.

Then he'd said, "You're making them scared, boy. The plans are working. They didn't lie. You are my ruthless heir. Keep at it."

"Here is your coffee, sir."

Taking the drink from my security guy, I gulped it back and set it on the tray. The heat from the brew burned down my throat. Hopefully, the caffeine would kick in fast.

I continued to scan the floor, stopping at a section with a large group of private security monitoring the players.

There, in the middle of the fray, I spotted her.

Breathtaking was all I could think to describe her. Her hair flowed loosely down her back, and her deep purple gown, though simple, clung to her every curve.

My stomach clenched as I took in the two pieces of jewelry she wore, a set of long earrings and a platinum cuff on her wrist. Two things I'd given her while on one of our secret trips.

I resisted the urge to run my fingers through my hair in frustration.

She knew what we had, and she still fought it.

Well, this time around, it was all or nothing. No matter how much it hurt. I couldn't do this on-off thing anymore.

"They look as if they are nearing the end of the play," Amir observed as he moved in to stand by me. "Do you think she is here for work or pleasure?" He answered his own question a second later. "I say work."

There were only three reasons Devani Maya Patel crossed The Library's threshold. To gamble, to work, or if she knew I planned to oversee the evening, to fuck.

Since Kir was the brother scheduled for tonight, the latter on the list wouldn't have crossed her mind.

She lifted a glass of champagne to her lips.

The fuck? I resisted the urge to stalk over and swipe the flute from her fingers. Then I noticed she never took a sip.

It looked as if Van was gracing us with her presence tonight.

She lifted the edges of her cards and gave them a noncommittal glance before making a comment that had the table laughing.

She weaved a wicked spell, dazzling men and women alike into losing concentration on the hands they played. She raised the stakes by twenty thousand by throwing in a handful of chips.

All but two players followed suit. Then she went higher, pushing it to a hundred grand. This left her with two other players.

Ahh. Now we had her victims. Leonard Gustov, a well-known fashion designer with ties to a Polish syndicate and the matriarch of the Sonnita Familia, Marianna Sonnita.

From my side, Amir observed. "Watching the queen in action is a masterclass in spying."

"When did she get here?"

"About two hours ago. Considering her future relationship status, this was the last place I expected her to show up. Before opening, Kir called and told me to reserve a table for Ms. Patel. I followed orders. What do you think she is up to?"

"It looks like she is preparing to stick a dagger into one of the two feral cats pretending to be kittens left in the game with her."

"I thought you should know. I worked freelance for her before I relocated to King Holdings. Sonnita is Interpol."

I loved the word freelance. It covered anything from hacker for hire to arms designer, as in Amir's case.

"Explains how her family gets away with the things they do."

Amir gestured to the room around us. "It does help to have people in the right places to protect our interests."

I smiled, hearing Arin's words on Amir's lips.

"I couldn't agree more."

By sending Rey into the CIA, Arin had ensured a way to navigate around scrutiny into some of our less-than-lawful activities. In exchange, access to King contacts allowed the agency to gain entry into our world, something they'd never be able to infiltrate without much time and effort.

"Should I set the usual private game for yourself and Ms. Patel?"

"No. That won't be necessary."

Confusion flashed over his face, and he opened his mouth as if to question me, then thought better of it and kept quiet.

"Are you planning to make rounds on the floor?"

"Absolutely. I'll wait until this play ends."

At that moment, Gustov glanced between the two women challenging him, narrowed his gaze, and then raised the pot by a cool five hundred thousand.

"He has nothing and is trying to buy his way into a win."

I smirked. "Gustov has no idea. Insulting their intelligence is the worst mistake he could make."

Sonnita matched, and then Devani re-raised by another five hundred thousand. Her face remained an impeccably smooth, composed mask as if she wasn't sitting in front of a pot worth nearly four million.

A tinge of sweat broke out over Gustov's forehead as he had to decide whether to fold and pay the debt he'd incurred or answer the challenge of Devani's call.

As if already knowing the outcome, Amir spoke into his wrist mic. "We are about to have a runner. Table three, with the diamond and winery queens."

Our security moved into position, ready to handle anything unexpected.

Sonnita commented on something, resulting in a smirk from Devani and Gustov's face reddening.

His Adam's apple bobbed as he swallowed, then he stood, throwing his cards down and exploding into an angry tirade.

Then his attention shifted to Devani.

All the hairs on the back of my neck stood up. This fucker had a serious death wish.

He reached over in an attempt to grab her cards. His hand barely grazed her when Devani pivoted, elbowing him in the chest and then punching him in the nose and throat. He collided against the table, and all of the other guests jumped away, not wanting to become collateral damage.

Next, Sonnita grabbed Gustov by the shirt, brought his bleeding face toward her, screamed something in Italian, and then kneed him in the stomach before taking his head and smacking it over and over into the stacks of chips.

The rage on both women's faces dared anyone to stop them from killing the fucker.

It also made it clear to everyone in the room that the two socialites were far from ornamental and definitely on the lethal side.

"Holy shit." Amir ran out of the observation area. "Why does this always happen on my shift?"

With a sigh, I shook my head and made my way into the gaming room behind him.

For the most part, the players remained at their tables. They continued their games as if nothing out of the ordinary had happened.

Well, except for those at Devani's table, of course. They congregated with their security personnel, watching the aftermath of their card game in morbid fascination.

In the club's ten-year history, we'd only had one major incident requiring club intervention.

Strike that. Now we had two.

One caused by Danika and the other by Devani. No wonder the patrons of the Library had named them the dynamic duo. One couldn't sit by while the other had all the fun.

I moved into the circle where club security stood, unsure how to handle the situation.

Devani clenched her fists tight, ready to land a few more strikes on the now immobile Gustov.

Sonnita's men surrounded her. No matter how hard they tried, they failed to calm her ire. From behind the wall they created, I heard a steady stream of nonsensical muttering about idiots who had no chance of winning against intelligently superior women and for dumbasses to keep their hands to themselves.

"Sir. The last time this occurred, it was only one of them to handle. And Mrs. King, as your family, was easier to console. These ladies are—" Amir paused, trying to gather the right words, "—on the more unpredictable side."

Maybe Amir forgot that Danika had nearly gutted the fucker who'd touched her. No, she had gutted him by slicing straight from above the groin up through the stomach. One of my men had to hold the idiot's intestines in until the emergency crew arrived.

"First, let's get Mr. Gustov moved to the holding room. Have first aid administered to ensure he won't die, but nothing more. While you keep Gustov in the world of the living, have our crew come in for cleanup. Also, make sure Ms. Sonnita remains as calm and comfortable as possible for the remainder of the evening."

"I take it you will handle your queen?"

My queen.

"You should know there is no such thing as handling a queen." I moved in Devani's direction.

Just as I was within a few feet of her, she turned, rage-filled, lust-glazed eyes boring into mine. Her face was flushed, and her breathing was measured and too controlled.

The way she held herself screamed that the refined socialite no longer existed and only a predator ready to pounce remained.

My body reacted as if she'd thrown down a gauntlet, and a primitive urge to dominate her coursed through me, making my cock swell.

"Why are you here?" she asked, licking her lips, making me think she imagined tasting mine.

"To escort you out of the gaming room." I gestured to Gustov. "That was some show."

"Let me repeat." She kept her words calm and measured. "Why are you here? Kir is the brother scheduled for shift tonight. I made sure of this."

So she wanted to avoid me. Too fucking bad.

"I gave him the night off." I stepped closer, her stance going stiff. "Now you answer the same question. Why are you here? Why aren't you at your event? Why aren't you announcing your engagement to another man?"

Her pupils dilated. "That's three questions."

"Fine, why aren't you with your fiancé?"

"No one has ever proposed to me, so how can I have a fiancé?"

"And whose choice was that?"

"None of your business." She jutted her chin up.

"And your reason for being here?"

"Same answer."

"I see." Stepping to the side, I motioned for her to move in front of me. "Let's continue our discussion somewhere else. The team needs to tidy up the floor display you created with Signora Sonnita."

Devani kept her penetrating focus on my face for a few seconds before she scanned the room, took in every detail around her, and swept past me.

Out of habit, I lifted my palm to set it on her lower back.

However, before my fingers touched her, she ordered, "Don't touch me."

"Why not, Highness?" I left my hand at a hover.

Her breath shifted, growing unsteady, her control slipping. My cock hardened further, becoming a heavy, uncomfortable weight in my pants.

"You aren't that dense." She ignored the people staring at her as she passed them in the lounge, and we made our way into the secured hallway leading to a set of elevators. "You know exactly why."

"Do I?" I asked when the cab doors opened, and we moved inside.

Reaching around her, I hit the club's lower-level button, and the elevator began its descent.

On purpose, I moved in behind her, crowding her and barely giving her space.

The flush in her skin deepened. "I wouldn't touch me if I were you. Not unless you plan to deliver."

"And what will you do, Director? If I touch you and leave you hanging?"

"I will—" she licked her lips, "—make your life very difficult."

"And how have you made it easy?" I shifted closer, letting my breath coast over her ear. "We are as tangled as things get."

She tilted her neck a fraction, and her eyes fluttered closed. "I mean it, Sam. Don't touch me. I have too much adrenaline pumping through my system. Since I couldn't kill that asshole in a room full of people, I need to either fuck or fight."

"What would you have done if Kir had been here instead of me?" I pressed my aroused body to her back, sandwiching her between me and the elevator's metal doors. "I doubt you would have given him the same options."

"Kir's worked with me before and knows how I operate. When I want space, he gives it to me."

"That doesn't answer my question. What kind of space would you need to get rid of the adrenaline? Would you find some poor replacement for me to burn off the energy in the sheets, or would you work it out in the gym?"

Her palms landed flat on the steel and flexed. "How I handle my needs is my own concern."

"Then you won't have any problems sharing, will you?" I scored my teeth along the sensitive skin of her shoulder and a whimper escaped her lips.

"Sam, you already know the answer."

"I want to hear you say it."

"I— I would go to the training facility."

"That's right, because beating the shit out of some defenseless recruit who underestimated your size is better than feeling dissatisfied in bed."

"W-why do you want me to say it? We have nothing more than sex, remember? Knowing details about my personal life isn't part of the equation."

"Ah, yes, we use each other to scratch the itch when the urge calls to us." I trailed my fingers up the side slit of her gown.

A shiver shook her body as goose bumps prickled her skin.

"Wouldn't you qualify this as an itch, Highness?" My fingers traced the edge of her underwear right before I slid underneath, grazed her swollen labia, and gripped her hip.

"T-this isn't about an itch. Not with the way I'm feeling."

"What is it about then?"

"If you don't know, then I'm better off going to the gym."

With my free hand, I twisted her hair around my palm and yanked her head back.

"Is that right?"

"Yes," she hissed.

The sound of a bell alerted us to the elevator arriving on the basement level. The doors opened into a dimly lit space.

"Sam, let me go." Arousal and passion-filled fury peered at me through her dark brown irises.

"Is that what you want?"

"I want to fuck or fight."

"Are those my only two choices?"

"That is all there is between us. Remember? No, correction. All we have is sex. Fuck me or let me go to the gym."

14

DEVANI

"YOU WANT TO FUCK, HIGHNESS?" SAM ASKED.

Lust raged in his golden gaze, making my heartbeat jump.

He had no idea how much I wanted him, needed him. How I wished he hadn't shown up tonight. The heart-to-heart with Neil had made it abundantly clear being anywhere near Sam would lead to trouble. I wasn't rational around him.

Now with this Gustov shit, I had no more logic left and only the endorphins running through my system.

Primal lust for this man fogged my brain, and he would either satisfy it or I'd find some other outlet.

In a quick twist of my shoulders and arms, I broke Sam's grip on my hair and body, grasped his arm, and faced him. "If I wasn't clear a second ago, let me clarify. I want to fuck so hard that I feel it with every step tomorrow. Can you satisfy my needs, or do I have to go beat the shit out of someone?"

Instead of answering, his attention shifted to my knuckles, red and raw from the punches I'd administered to Gustov's face. Something inside me felt a sense of satisfaction from giving that piece of shit a beatdown for believing he had a right to touch me because he lost a poker game.

No, it was because he'd lost to a woman. Considering his line of work, I guessed his ego couldn't handle it.

To be a fly on the wall when he learned the real reason for tonight's invitation and his new living situation. A holding cell in one of the storage caves of Marianna's vineyard.

"Your hand needs attention." The deep rasp in Sam's voice shot a wave of arousal straight to my core, heightening the need pumping through my body.

I leaned forward, bringing my nose a hairsbreadth from his.

"Mr. King, in real-life fights, even queens get scrapes and cuts. Protecting our hands in gloves and fighting in cages for sport in hopes of winning a bet is considered child's play." I bit his lower lip hard enough to sting before releasing it. "But you wouldn't know these things. Well, maybe once upon a time you did, but now you're a King and like competing in underground matches and such."

He narrowed his gaze. "You're playing a dangerous game right now, Highness."

"Do I look scared?" I asked, meeting his glare.

I wasn't sure what was coming over me. Maybe I wanted to fight *and* fuck.

He gripped my hips in an almost too-painful hold and walked me backward. "You asked for it."

"I sure hope so."

My breath grew shallow, knowing exactly where we were going.

Licking my lips, I asked, "Are you taking me in for an interrogation?"

"I doubt you'd divulge any information, even if we were."

From the stories Sam had told me when Arin had originally bought the building, he'd used the room to extract information.

Once The Library had come into existence, it had become a private gaming room.

Sam had it renovated to something resembling the style of an upscale speakeasy. He'd claimed it for exclusive use for his clients who wanted a personal touch, including those who couldn't have associations in public but needed to meet without scrutiny.

Once inside the room, he only switched on one light, casting the space in a dim glow.

He positioned me with my back pushed against a hard granite counter.

"If I recall, there was a time or two you used this room to extract a few secrets out of me."

A lump formed in my throat. Why had I brought that up? Those memories were too intimate, too personal, and too painful.

His expression grew hard, and he said, "Let's not kid ourselves, Highness. It was all an illusion in the guise of sex."

I held in a sharp breath at the coldness of his words, refusing to let him know how much they hurt.

Instead, I nipped his jaw with my teeth and stated, "You're an asshole."

"And you're a manipulative bitch." He laughed, cupping my throat and giving me the deliciously wicked pressure he knew I craved. "We established this a long time ago."

My breath grew shallow, and a low whimper escaped my lips. "Are we going to keep talking or are you planning to fuck me?"

"I'll get to fucking you when I'm good and ready. You walked into my place and caused problems tonight. Now, you'll deal with the consequences."

"The hell I will."

With speed I hadn't expected, he captured my wrists in one hand.

His attention went to the cuff on my wrist, the one with our names on it.

Instead of commenting, he unlatched the clip and set the bracelet to the side.

He tugged the bowtie free from his neck and used it to tie my wrists together. Then he lifted me onto the counter and secured my bound hands above my head to a metal fixture that had once held the heavy chain for an antique chandelier.

Shit. He had me stretched out like a sacrifice.

He pushed the slit of my gown open, and it took all my strength not to squirm. "Is your pussy wet from the beatdown you gave to the idiot or the fact you know I saw it, Highness?"

I would not give him the satisfaction of knowing the truth, of knowing when I'd seen him, felt his presence, all I could think of was him—of him touching me, taking me, being his.

The case no longer mattered. All my plans no longer mattered. All I wanted was him.

"You give yourself too much credit."

Cupping me through my soaked underwear, he circled my clit with his thumb, and I couldn't help but gasp. "I know this body inside and out. Probably better than you do."

"The hell you do." I tried to clamp my thighs together to no avail. "Forget it. I changed my mind. I don't want to fuck you anymore. I'd rather punch someone. Get me down."

"And become a victim of the punch? Not a chance." He pushed my underwear to the side and thrust two fingers deep into my sopping pussy.

Stars flashed behind my eyelids as my back bowed and my vaginal walls clamped down on his pistoning fingers.

"You demanded to fuck. We're going to fuck, Highness."
He wrapped his free hand around my throat and jaw and
leaned forward.

I licked my lips and let my eyes flutter closed as his
breath coasted over my mouth in anticipation of a searing
kiss.

"Just know, this is all on my terms. Not yours. I've
marked you, inside and out."

What the hell could he mean by that?

Instead of allowing me to linger too long on his words,
he increased the rhythm of his fingers, pumping in and out
of my core. He worked me until tiny spasms wrenched
through me.

Just as I flew over the crest, he murmured, "This is why
no other man will ever satisfy you as I can. No matter how
much you don't want to admit it, I'm fucking
irreplaceable."

Dazed and overwhelmed by the cascade of pleasure
coursing through every inch of me, I ignored his words
and rode out my release.

When I finally stopped convulsing, he withdrew from
my soaked channel and brought his wet fingers to my lips.
"Suck."

I followed his command, letting my spicy essence fill
my mouth. Less than a second later, he covered my lips
with his.

This possessive, unforgiving kiss overwhelmed me,
intoxicated me, made my whole being crave all of him. He
angled my head to meet the demands of his mouth while

massaging the column of my throat with rhythmic squeezes designed to heighten my pleasure.

I wanted to pull him closer and push him away, knowing at the end of this we would go our separate ways. But I had no control over this situation, bound and at his mercy.

This was his punishment, his reminder of all I'd thrown away.

He broke our embrace and stared at me with pupils so large, they ate up his irises, turning them into thin rings of gold.

"Sam, we need to stop this. I don't want to hurt you more than I already have." As soon as those words left my lips, I regretted them.

I revealed too much. I'd made myself too vulnerable.

Holding my gaze, his hands glided down my body, took hold of my underwear, and slid them off my hips and down my legs before throwing them to the side. "Stop lying to yourself. We know damn well it's not me you're trying to protect."

"You don't know anything."

"Oh, I know plenty." He slid to the floor and dropped my knees over his shoulders, bringing my exposed core flush to his face. "I'm the only one to get past your defenses." He blew on my heated, swollen flesh, making me squirm. "I'm the only one who makes you crave more." He licked from my slick core to my aching clit, causing a whimper to escape my lips. "I'm the only one you give your complete trust and control."

"Don't." I turned my face away, unable to hear the truth of his words.

"Facts are facts, Highness." His mouth descended on my pussy, and all coherent thoughts left my mind.

I moaned and gasped as he gorged on me as a man starved. He circled and worried the sensitive bundle of nerves at the apex of my sex. At the same time, his fingers plunged and rubbed against the spot deep inside my core meant to drive my desire high and higher.

I couldn't think, only feel the onslaught of sensations through my system.

Everything inside me clenched and flexed as heat built. Still, release seemed out of reach.

I needed more. Just something more.

I jerked against my restraints, hearing the metal post creak with the ferocity of my tugs.

"Fuck, I love those sounds you make," he murmured as he nipped my labia.

"Sam. God. Bite me right there. Stop the torture. Make it hurt. I don't want to feel or think anymore."

He paused for a second, lifting his face, watching me, assessing me.

Then in the next second, his fingers thrust knuckles-deep into my pussy, scissoring in and out, unrelenting.

"That's not what this is about. You wanted me. That's what you will get."

"Dammit, Sam. You know I need it."

The pain would push away the emotion. The last thing I wanted was the emotion of this all.

"What you need is to come." His mouth returned to my core as he altered the rhythm of his thrusts.

Almost immediately, the breath left my body, and I arched up as my vaginal walls clamped down on his pumping digits. My back bowed, and my pussy clenched and released. I tossed my head side to side, muttering nonsensical words, lost completely in pleasure.

Rising to his feet, Sam pushed down his pants, letting his cock spring free. After taking hold of the thick root of his erection, he positioned the weeping head at the slick opening of my pussy, and drove to the hilt.

"Sheer heaven," he groaned.

I couldn't respond, my barely waned orgasm reigniting. Nothing felt like this man. I couldn't get enough of him.

Reaching above me, he untied my wrists, and I immediately wrapped my arms around his neck.

"I want it hard. I need it harder." I closed my eyes, bringing myself flush against his body. "Give me what only you can."

"Devani, you make no sense." Bringing one hand between us, he cupped my jaw and throat and kissed me.

My legs tightened around his waist. "I make sense to myself. Just do it. Please, I'm desperate."

"How can I deny my queen when she begs so beautifully for her king."

I stiffened, realizing what I'd done. I'd begged. What I'd promised him I'd never do that night when he'd been such an asshole to me.

However, before I could respond, he pulled out and

RUTHLESS HEIR

slammed in with a vicious thrust that had me seeing stars and needing more.

My nails dug into his shoulders, and I cried out, "Yes, like that. Give me more."

After that, there was nothing between us but our bodies' brutal, carnal desires. My teeth raked across Sam's skin, and he fucked into me with hard, relentless drives of his cock.

We were two people possessed. The rage and the onslaught of emotions from the last week purging through our physical needs.

Slowly, another orgasm rose up with small quivers in my pussy and then spasms.

"Oh, God, Sam. I'm there."

I threw my head back, arching. My vaginal muscles clamped down hard and released in a dance around his pistoning cock, over and over.

Fisting my hair, he brought my mouth to his as his release washed over him, and he shot hot and hard inside my trembling pussy.

15

Devani

I closed my eyes and leaned against my shower wall, letting the spray pound my body. Hopefully, the steaming water would help wash away whatever caused this crud that seemed to have attached itself to me like the plague.

This freaking made no sense. For the last three weeks, my hours were long, but I'd slept at home.

Why couldn't I shake this exhaustion?

Fuck. The last thing I needed was to have caught some type of bug.

How was that even possible? I was up to date on all my vaccines and had regular checkups.

This was what I got for making fun of Neil about the malaria incident. But honestly, he'd been a total baby about the whole thing.

I could only imagine the looks on Neil's and Noah's faces when they learned I'd gone to the doctor for anything other than an injury resulting from a gunshot or a knife wound. They'd give me shit for days.

A private physician who made house calls was probably a better bet.

This way, I could keep things quiet until I knew if I'd gotten some superbug or just a cold.

If it ended up being something as stupid as a cold, I swore I'd scream.

I'd taken an assignment the day after a shooting injury. More than once.

Okay, I had to get out of my head and make the call instead of wasting time guessing.

Turning off the shower, I dried my body, wrapped a towel around my head, and stepped into the heated primary bathroom of my bedroom suite.

Another wave of nausea rushed through me. And this constant queasiness. What was up with that?

Maybe I shouldn't have eaten that pizza so late last night.

I always felt better after a hard training session. I'd head to the gym and beat the shit out of some poor recruit, as Sam had said a few nights ago.

And God. What the fuck was I doing with him?

I knew better, but I'd let my hormones and adrenaline overtake my logic.

My body hummed, remembering the way he'd taken me. He'd definitely taken the edge off from the Gustov incident.

But everything had come back in full force the moment I'd decided to arrange today's meeting with the King brothers. I had no doubt being in a room with Sam would play havoc with my already messed-up body.

Maybe I deserved this for drawing him and his brothers into my plans.

Technically, they'd *fallen* into the plans. If Sam hadn't owned the company I'd competed with to buy up all the debts behind the Circle of Ten, then the Kings wouldn't be anywhere near this mission.

Outside of Shah and being pieces of shit as a whole, I couldn't understand what the Circle could have done to any of the Kings to make the Kings go after them.

But if I asked, then I would have to divulge the same information.

Better Sam and I lived on opposite sides of this unsaid line he set in the sand.

Be his in the open, or it would be as I'd initially set the rules: fuck and walk away.

Maybe, if he'd pushed sooner before I'd gone down this road, I'd have altered my plans.

I couldn't lie to myself. Killing Ashok Shah had sat top on my priority list from the moment I'd fallen for Sam. I'd known very few people who could get away with eliminating assholes while leaving no trace, and I was one of them.

Too late to think of what-ifs. In life, going backward helped no one.

Sighing, I pulled the towel from my hair, laid it across a drying rack, and approached the mirror above the double sink.

Suddenly, my heart skipped a beat as I stared at my reflection. Leaning forward, I studied my body.

Were my boobs bigger? Not just bigger, huge.

What the hell— No, that wasn't possible.

I'd noticed my dresses feeling tight in the chest but assumed I needed to cut down on eating whole cakes and reduce the number of desserts I ate with Danika when she indulged her pregnancy cravings.

But that couldn't explain the constant tenderness or extra sensitivity in my breasts.

A pressure built in my chest, unlike anything I had ever felt. I braced my arms on the counter, closing my eyes for a brief moment.

Oh God. Oh God. Oh God.

Not now. Not ever. I'd accepted it wasn't a scenario for my future.

This couldn't be happening, especially with all the shit going on in my life, with the plans I'd just affirmed.

I had no problem risking myself for an assignment, but now...

My fingers tightened on the counter as my knees grew weak.

No. I was jumping the gun. It could still be the flu or mother nature fucking with my cycle. I was religious about staying on the maintenance schedule for my birth control.

The failure rate for the shot sat in the range of less than one percent.

Plus, I rarely had a period with this contraceptive, just spotting.

Which I'd had.

Nothing was true until I took a test to confirm my suspicions.

A tear slipped down my cheek.

Who was I kidding?

I knew my body. I knew the truth. No matter how much I wanted to pretend otherwise, all my symptoms pointed to one conclusion: it wasn't a cold.

What was I going to do?

I lifted my head, facing my reflection again.

Oh, God. I had to tell Sam.

Dread settled in my gut. He never wanted children. He'd made a vow never to let Shah's blood taint another soul.

Now, one potentially grew in my belly.

I slid my hand over my stomach as an image of my parents and brother appeared in my mind. A part of them lived here too. A kernel of hope bloomed for the first time since my family died, knowing a piece of them would go on.

Was this how Sam's mom had felt when she found out she was pregnant?

No. I'm sure it was completely different and a million times scarier. I couldn't even fathom the pain and sorrow she must have felt.

Her family had thrown her out for getting pregnant and shaming them in their strict Indo-American community. Ashok Shah had promised her the world, used her, and then rejected her for a lucrative marriage.

She'd been alone with nowhere to go and no means to raise a child on her own. Instead, from everything I learned about her, she gathered the strength to raise her son while working two jobs and living with two other single moms.

If only she'd known the danger she'd been in from her ex.

Suddenly, a fear like nothing I'd ever felt surged through me, followed by anger.

I'd spent my whole life a target. I never had the luxury to trust a soul because of my uncles and their greed. I refused to let my child have a day like that. I'd protect them with every ounce of my being.

Though to do that, I had to stay alive.

Which meant no one besides Sam could know about my pregnancy.

For a split second, the thought of keeping everything to myself crossed my mind, and then I pushed it to the side. If Sam truly was anything like Ashok Shah, I'd have done it in a heartbeat. Then again, I wouldn't have fallen for him or slept with him in the first place.

Knowing I had to reach out to him, I grabbed my phone from the counter and dialed his number.

"Do we need to scratch an itch before our meeting this morning?"

God, how was I going to face him while holding this

secret? How would I sit across from him and pretend as if our lives weren't permanently changed?

Ignoring his question, I said, "We need to talk."

"We don't talk. We fuck."

I gritted my teeth. "You may not want to fuck me after I give you some information."

"I'll take that as a challenge."

"You take everything as a challenge."

"With you, yes." The humor in his tone annoyed me and gave me a sense of dread.

"This isn't a game, Sam."

"Of course, it is. You started it. I'm just keeping everything in play."

"Stop with the poker metaphors. Can you meet me or not?"

"We are meeting. In a few hours, in fact. Your company arranged it."

"Just say no instead of being an ass."

He remained quiet for a moment, then asked, "Can I assume this isn't going to be in public?"

"We need to be alone." A lump formed in my throat. "For what I have to tell you, it's the best."

"For you or me?"

"Both of us."

"I see."

"No. You don't have a clue."

"Now, I'm intrigued. I suppose you're going to meet Joshi for casino night at the Andhi tonight?"

"How do you know my schedule?"

"I know everything about you, Highness. Will the Andhi Hotel work?"

"Yes."

"Meet me in the theatre dressing lounge. It's always locked, but I'm sure you'll find a way inside."

16

SAM

"READY TO DROP THE HAMMER?" NIK ASKED AS HE ROCKED back in his chair next to me.

We sat in the palatial conference room of Rawal, Zane & Mitchell, the law firm Jesika Rawal managed with her partners. As a favor, she'd granted us space to conduct our meeting today, which gave us anonymity when it came to getting our prey to the table.

"This is but one piece of the puzzle. No need to drop any hammer when things implode on their own." I scrolled through the stocks on my phone. "Besides, we have a meeting before that one to clear."

"If Jay and Dani catch wind of this, they will have our balls." Kir shot Nik a warning glance.

Today, I'd call in debts for a group who had no idea I'd

purchased their outstanding loans for properties they'd never developed.

Typically, the debt-collector role in the company fell to Kir as the enforcer of King Holdings. But since this group had a personal connection to me and, therefore, the entire King family, all four brothers were in house.

This connection dated back to the fateful day I'd met Nik and Kir. The day I'd become so desperate to find a safe place to stay, I'd believed a nice couple who'd offered me a sanctuary.

It had never sat well with Arin that I was the only one of the four of us targeted by the group for kidnapping. He'd researched and eventually traced the building owners to a person tied to Shah and Joshi. In our world, there were no coincidences, especially when removing the evidence of crimes. And I was the most significant proof of Shah's crimes.

"Separation of church and state," Rey interjected. "They know the rules. We don't interfere in their business, and they don't get involved in ours."

"Says the man who tells his wife every-fucking-thing." I smirked.

"Considering her former line of work, you can't hide anything from her. So you might as well come clean from the beginning. Besides, she helps watch our backs as much as Dani does."

Rey's words weren't an understatement. King Holdings' interests remained under lock and key between Danika and Lilly. Two internationally wanted hackers with skills to boggle the mind came in handy, especially when protecting the information we wanted kept secured from the world.

"Which of us is going to take the lead?" Kir's focus landed on me.

Nik answered, "This is Sam's field of expertise. Let him handle it."

"Like he handled the club the other night?" Rey lifted a brow. "The cleaning bill for one night seemed higher than normal."

My lips curved as I remembered the way Devani and I had separated after fucking each other's brains out.

We'd barely caught our breaths before she pushed me back and said she planned to go home. The intensity of what we'd shared had left her raw, and her instincts pushed her to run. So I let her. Though before she opened the door, I took her wrist and clasped the cuff back into place. She knew what it meant, whether she wanted to admit it or not.

It was all a matter of waiting. It seemed as if that was all I did nowadays.

Maybe the phone call from earlier in the morning meant what I thought it did, or maybe I was fooling myself.

Focusing back on Rey's statement, I said, "Sometimes we have patrons who choose to run and others who object to that behavior."

"Fuck. I knew I shouldn't have let you take the shift. Why didn't you call us when everything went down?"

"Because I had my hands full. Just be happy it didn't turn into a shutdown as I dealt with in Danika's situation."

"Then I'm sure you know your queen isn't engaged?" Nik focused on me in his knowing way.

"Can anyone claim a queen?"

Nik smirked. "A King can."

At that moment, the conference room opened, and Devani walked in with a contingent of three women and one man as representatives from Maya Ratna Holdings.

Immediately, my blood and body stirred. The woman before me carried herself not like the Solon weapon but a corporate shark ready to battle. Good thing she'd come as one of the debt owners and not as opposition.

She held my gaze for the briefest of seconds as she strode to her seat across the table from my brothers and me. Something I could only describe as worry flashed in her dark eyes before she schooled it away and replaced it with her cool, collected confidence.

"Tell me again that you haven't claimed her," Nik whispered. "A blind man could see what's between the two of you."

"It doesn't count unless she accepts it."

"So what? You're giving up?"

"It's all or nothing."

"Everyone says I'm the one most like Arin, but they have it all wrong. It's you. You've always followed his playbook. So I take it you plan to make her come to you? And if she doesn't, you'll walk away?"

"As I said, all or nothing."

Once everyone took their seats, we made the preliminary introductions and began the meeting.

"As per the brief my assistant sent you—" I gestured to a set of documents in front of us, "—we thought it only fair to disclose that Rex Consolidated is one of the financing subsidiaries of King Holdings."

Alana Tran, Maya Ratna's CEO, smiled. "I should have figured it out with the name Rex. That is Latin for king. Am I correct?"

"Our father enjoyed using every version of our name for his businesses." Nik returned her amusement.

"You've put me in an awkward position, considering my relationship with some of the parties joining your meeting today." Devani leaned forward in her chair.

"Business is business, Ms. Patel. Otherwise, you wouldn't have bought the other half of the debt for these businesses." I lifted a brow.

I still couldn't figure out what she gained by acquiring outstanding loans and bonds for Shah, Joshi, and his circle. I had my reasons, but she had none as far as I knew.

"Out of curiosity, how did you learn about us?" Alana asked. "We work very hard to create an invisible footprint."

Before I could respond, Devani answered, "Lilly Lennox."

"King," Rey corrected. "She's a King now."

Alana glanced at Devani, shook her head, and then muttered, "She was ours first. Where's her loyalty?"

Well, well, even in her company, she had Solon agents planted. Then I scanned the other members of Devani's team. I should have noticed how they sized things up when they stepped into the room.

The cop eyes. Solon, all of them.

Devani lived and breathed her organization.

Was there even a chance for us in the long run?

"She's dickmatized." Rey chuckled, bringing me out of my thoughts. "Isn't that what you said I did to her and why she caused you so much trouble last year?"

Devani's dark eyes lifted to mine, and a surge of energy pulsed between us.

"Among other things, Agent King." Devani shifted her attention to the folder in front of her. "Gentlemen, I believe I have a counteroffer to keep my affiliation with this deal anonymous."

"Wish to keep your hands clean for your future father-in-law?" I kept my tone even but allowed the barb to strike.

Then almost instantly regretted it when a crease formed between her brows, and her lips tightened for fraction of a second. I never allowed my emotions to push to the surface in any business dealings, and this small infraction told me how much her call had left me off-kilter.

"Something like that. Now to my proposal."

Less than fifteen minutes later, I scanned the faces of my brothers, expecting some sort of reaction to Devani's proposal. She'd proposed to sell all of the outstanding debt to us for a dollar with the condition we make it look as if her uncles were the ones behind the sale without implicating her in any way.

She'd literally handed me everything I'd wanted for the last ten years on a silver platter.

Why?

This couldn't be just about the case.

"One last question before we break to discuss your proposal." I held Devani's dark gaze.

A surge of something buzzed between us. Maybe it was all the things we'd left unsaid.

"Go ahead."

"Why are you giving us such a large portfolio? What is it you are after?"

A calculating curve touched her full lips, reminding me of other things she'd done with them. As if she'd sensed where my thought drifted, she licked them.

"Those are two questions. But to answer, all you need to know is this saying: The foundation of a building is only as strong as its weakest links."

"And your uncles are the links?" Nik asked.

She held my stare as she rubbed her thumb over her knuckles. "No. Sam helped with that situation the other night. My uncles are the sledgehammer to crack the whole foundation."

Well, that confirmed a suspicion I had all along. Somehow, we'd fallen into one of her many Solon strategies.

Instead of being pissed, I wanted to find the closest office and fuck her senseless.

"Let's take a twenty-minute recess." Nik smacked my

back, breaking the connection with Devani. "This will allow us plenty of time to return with an answer."

Devani nodded, her expression giving nothing away.

I rose from my chair. Nik, Kir, and Rey followed. We moved into a small office, each of us taking a position at various spots in the room.

Rey spoke first, directing his words to me. "Should we have left the room so you two could fuck?"

"Asshole."

He shrugged. "Doesn't change what we saw. If her people didn't know you were together, they do now."

"We aren't together."

Kir moved toward me as if to punch me. "What the fuck is wrong with you?"

"We will get to that."

Kir glared at me.

Nik stepped between us and said, "You make the call on this deal. This is your game. We'll support what you decide."

Before he put the decision on me, I had to let them know about Devani's motives.

"You do realize she's working a case and using us to manipulate her plans?"

Rey moved next to Kir, pulling him back against the wall where he leaned. "Van wouldn't have the reputation she does if she wasn't two steps ahead of everyone. Remember, I was a victim of one of her brilliant maneuvers not long ago."

"You walked right into it like a chump," Kir reminded him.

"I got the girl in the end, so that's all that matters."

"You weren't so calm about it at the time."

I still remembered the day he'd come back from an assignment and found Danika's new art appraiser working in the gallery. Devani had maneuvered Lilly into a job without letting anyone know she was Rey's ex.

To describe it as a clusterfuck was an understatement.

"Let's say time has given me a different perspective," Rey mused.

"Meaning?"

"Her motives for her ulterior plans are never about herself. In fact, she rarely considers her safety. If she did, she wouldn't take half the risks she does."

"Do you know something?" I asked.

"I know a lot of things. My question is, does it matter if you have all the answers? Your woman is here, needs us to assist her, and you're the one who gets to make the call."

"If you even think about saying she isn't your woman, I swear to God, I'll punch you in the face right now." The anger in Kir's voice and how he clenched his fist made me pause.

He knew about the baby.

"Can I assume Jay told you?"

"Our wives kept the information from us. Not very fair to use their love for you to hold secrets." Nik leaned back against a desk. "We only know because we walked in on a conversation they were having."

I turned to Rey. "And does Lilly know?"

"She suspected weeks ago. She said something about testing fate and inevitability, but I hadn't taken it seriously."

"And you didn't think to give me a heads-up about it?"

"What did you expect me to say? Hey, jackass, you know how my wife believes in all the woo-woo, fate stuff. Well, she says since you don't wrap it up, she thinks you knocked up your spy girlfriend."

"You're an asshole."

"Who's the asshole for keeping us in the dark?" Rey folded his arms across his chest. "We're your brothers. Did you think we wouldn't have your back?"

"What could any of you do when I have no control over this?"

Everything in my gut said the meeting tonight revolved around the pregnancy.

But what would she say?

I'd spent so much time telling her I never wanted children. Would she believe me if I told her I wanted our child?

Fuck. I was jumping the gun.

"Does this weigh on your decision for her proposal?" Kir asked, circling back to the main topic of discussion, his anger still visible on his face.

"No. I keep business and personal separate."

Rey grunted, telling me he thought I was full of shit.

"Is that a yes, then?" Nik probed.

"You realize we are letting her move us around like one of her chess pieces? Hopefully, it won't bite us in the ass."

"Did you forget, chess is a Solon agent's favorite game, and Devani is the best? The objective is to protect the king." Rey smiled as he twisted his wedding band. "Lilly shot me to keep me safe. Imagine what your queen would do if things didn't go according to plan."

I sighed and moved toward the door. "At least something very rare will come out of this deal."

"What's that?" Kir asked.

I smiled. "Not only will the Queen of Diamonds owe me a favor, so will the Director of Solon North America."

"Wouldn't we owe her for selling to us?" Kir studied me.

"No. To keep her name out of all actions against the Circle requires time and money. What we want is out in the open. Her activities require discretion. Extra precautions come at a price. And a queen likes to accrue debts, not incur them."

"And let me guess, you plan to collect."

"Of course."

A LITTLE BEFORE SEVEN IN THE EVENING, I STEPPED OUT OF my car and onto the streets of a neighborhood I'd despised as a child. Here, I'd spent the first fourteen years of my life. This was where Nik, Kir, Rey, and I ran around, making nuisances of ourselves. The place where we'd bonded with the young Danika and created our own makeshift family to replace the ones we'd lost.

I inclined my head to a group of kids who checked me out from head to toe. Suspicion lit their eyes exactly as I'd watched Arin the first time I saw him. I couldn't understand why some rich fucker with bodyguards would enter the neighborhood.

Now, I was the rich fucker walking the same streets.

I smiled inside and thought of how Arin would have laughed his ass off.

Except these kids wouldn't dare rob me. Well, most of them. After Nik, Kir, Rey, and I started making Arin's vision a reality, we'd come back to help everyone who wanted it. From jobs to revitalizing the neighborhood to a safe place to live.

Though there were still those who refused to take anything from the former gang kids.

I made my way into a tall, renovated brick apartment building and up four flights of stairs to an apartment guarded by four King Holdings security members.

They opened the door, and I walked inside. On a far sofa sat a couple I knew every minute detail about.

Kala and Nimesh Barot.

The asshole's butler and head chef.

Fear flashed over their faces as I came into view, making me want to sigh. What the fuck had Shah done to them in his house?

Then I thought of how things had gone down in the meeting this afternoon.

When Shah had arrived with Joshi and five of his partners, he thought he'd get to charm his way into a renegotiation of loans.

Then when he saw us sitting on the other side of the table, I almost thought his head would explode right then and there.

Now the King brothers not only controlled all of his debts incurred before Jayna had taken over his finances, but also the outstanding loans and bonds for the new ventures he'd created. There was no Shah International 2.0 for him.

I held my hands up in a gesture of surrender as I moved into the room. *"I'm not going to hurt you. I owe you a debt for caring for Jayna and Danika when they were young."*

"They were children." Kala watched me, wariness still in her gaze. *"We did what we could."* She dropped her head and wrung her hands. *"Sometimes, it wasn't enough."*

"Jayna would disagree. Can I ask why you reached out today? You could have called us long ago." I took the seat across from them.

Nimesh answered, *"Sir has information on your family."* He paused as if trying to gather his words. *"He is part of something we cannot condone."*

"That doesn't answer my question. Why today?"

"It is no longer safe for us in that house. He made threats to the staff and had our rooms searched. He believes all of us are traitors. He said we helped the Patel brothers sell him out to you. The other things I won't repeat." Anger radiated from Nimesh.

"*After all these years of service, he treated me as if I were garbage.*"

"*Did he find anything in your room?*"

"*No. When we learned Sir's secret, I started sending things with my children when they visited.*" Kala picked up a satchel, opened it, and pulled out a phone. "*This is the only item we have ever stolen from him. At this point, it no longer matters if he tracks it.*"

"*May I?*" I asked, reaching for the mobile.

"*Go to the pictures. They will tell you all you need to know. The information on the Circle of Ten, the horrible things they do, your family, your history, and your brother.*"

"*Brothers,*" I corrected.

Kala shook her head. "*Not the Kings. You and Jayna have a brother.*"

17

DEVANI

A LITTLE AFTER ELEVEN IN THE EVENING, I MADE MY WAY into the dressing lounge of the theatre room at the Andhi New York City. This was the crown jewel property in the hotel division of Shah International. The place where the Shah legacy in the United States had started.

Even forty years after its grand opening, it was one of the prime hotels in the city, with impeccable service and old-world style. And only a handful of people knew every inch of it belonged to someone other than Ashok Shah.

Soon it would be in the rightful owner's hands. But then again, new secrets would come to life: Neil, Sam, and Jayna, three siblings born out of so much tragedy.

I dropped my head.

How the fuck was I going to ensure it now?

No matter what, I had to see this through. It would happen even if I wasn't the one to pull the trigger. The bastards would die.

I'd get Sam his revenge. I'd get Neil his revenge.

When I heard footsteps approaching, I adjusted the bracelets on my wrist, deactivating the microchips designed to record and send conversations to the central data collection center. Then as a backup, I set my clutch on a dressing counter and activated a scrambling device designed to block all communications in and out of the room.

"This conversation must be super secret if you are getting all high-tech." Sam entered from the room's shadows, wearing dark pants and a button-down gray shirt rolled up at the sleeves.

He should have looked out of place in such an elegant room and with me in a formal gown, but he fit in. As if he owned the place.

"It's important and needs to remain a secret."

"That sounds ominous." He moved closer to me, then paused when I started backing away. "If you're here to tell me we can't see each other, save your breath. The rules are we fuck and go our merry way. If you decide to stop hiding, you know where I am. I'm no longer investing anything more than necessary in whatever this is between us."

I closed my eyes for a brief second and then said, "What I'm about to say is to inform you only. You made your feelings on this situation clear a long time ago."

"Go on." He watched me as if he were a predator ready to pounce. "I'm a big boy. I can take anything you throw my way."

"I'm pregnant."

The air in the room stilled as if frozen in place.

Sam stared at me, not moving, not speaking. The only indication he heard what I'd said was the intense play of emotions burning in his eyes.

When he remained quiet, I pushed, "Say something."

"I know."

"What do you mean, you know? Know what?"

"That you're pregnant."

"How the fuck would you know when I didn't? I confirmed it earlier today."

He moved toward me, not stopping until he had me by the waist, and then walked me backward, pinning my back to the wall.

"Oh, I have a whole list. Would you like to hear it?"

The ferocity of his words had my heartbeat accelerating.

"Umm. Go right ahead."

"I pay attention to you. I notice everything about you. I've watched things changing for the last month, especially these." He cupped my breast.

Out of instinct, I arched into his hold.

"Also, you're never tired to the point of utter exhaustion. I've seen you go for weeks with the barest amount of sleep and then find me for an all-night sex session. You have more energy than anyone I have ever met. If I could bottle it, I'd be the richest man in the world."

He slid one hand to my nape, tilting my face up. "Then the big one. The one that confirmed it for me was after that night in my penthouse."

"You mean, the night I should have neutered your ass?"

"Yes, that one." His lips curved slightly. "Highness, when you're pissed, you walk away without a backward glance. You are cold, calculating, and have no problems freezing anyone out. You never let anyone see your emotions and especially let them know if anything they said landed or hurt you. Yet that night, I watched all of my words hit their mark. And the cherry on top, you cried. You do not cry. Ever. You left my place and broke down in the passageway."

I tried to jerk my face away, refusing to let him see how much his analysis gutted me. "Take your psycho-babble and stuff it. You don't know me."

"At this moment." He cupped my throat with his other hand and pressed his front to mine. "I know you better than you do."

"Then you're positive the baby is yours?" My heartbeat accelerated.

He narrowed his gaze and leaned in until his mouth was a hairsbreadth from mine. "I never had a single doubt."

"What makes you so sure?" My question came out through a shallow breath as his fingers flexed on my neck.

"Because you're mine." He bit my lower lip. "You were

mine from the moment you sauntered up to my table that first night and threw down that challenge."

"You think too highly of yourself."

"It doesn't change the facts, Highness. When I said I marked you inside and out, I wasn't talking about our child. I meant that I'm in your soul. You'd rather burn off your energy in the gym than even imagine someone other than me touching you, tasting you, being with you. Sooner or later, you'll have to admit the truth."

"You don't know what you're talking about."

"Keep lying to yourself." His mouth sealed over mine.

Without thought, I met his demands, needing to feel him and accept what was happening in our lives.

In the back of my mind, logic screamed that the conversation wasn't even close to halfway done, that his words warned of too many consequences, that we had too much on the line.

Instead of listening to my voice of reason, I pushed it aside, wanting nothing more than to lose myself in the man before me.

My fingers went to the buttons of his shirt.

Sam drew me forward and then worked the hidden zipper at the back of my dress while continuing his intoxicating assault on my lips.

This need felt different, almost desperate. I couldn't get to his skin fast enough. He toed off his shoes as I pulled his shirt from the waist of his pants. My fingers moved up his chest, unfastening the buttons, and then pushed the cotton material over his tattooed shoulders and arms.

Next went his belt, pants, and underwear, pooling at his feet.

My gown fell in a similar heap on the floor, leaving me clad in only a thong, thigh-high stockings, and four-and-a-half-inch heels.

Sam's eyes seared me, and his pupils dilated, turning his amber irises into rings of gold. My nipples beaded into tight points, and a flood of desire pooled between my legs. It took effort not to squirm and press my thighs together.

"I have no idea how you haven't noticed your breasts until now." He cupped one, pinching the tip and eliciting a whimper from my lips.

I grabbed hold of his shoulders. "I've— I've been a bit preoccupied."

"Apparently." Sam released my breast, lifted me into his arms, and carried me to an oversized couch in the corner of the room.

He sat, settling my knees to straddle his thighs. His palms slid up my back, causing goose bumps to prickle my skin in the wake of his hands. I tilted my head as his mouth and fingers trailed over my collarbone, grazing the area where his mark lay hidden under the makeup.

He lifted his head, gazing at me with such emotion, tears burned the back of my throat.

How were we going to navigate all this?

Everything was so fucked-up, and there was no guarantee on how this would play out.

I couldn't overthink it. I had to enjoy the time I had with him.

Gripping his shoulder, I drew him to me, sealing our lips together and losing myself in the intoxication of his mouth and touch.

I jerked as he tore my underwear from my hips.

"I have plans for this pussy."

His fingers delved lower to the lips of my sex. He parted me and plunged two fingers deep as his thumb circled my clit.

I couldn't help but moan and gasp with each thrust of his hand.

When he added the third, I bucked against him, rode him. My mind clouded, wanting desperately for his cock to replace his fingers.

"Sam, I need you in me."

"I am in you."

"Your cock. I need your cock."

"Then put me in." He lifted me, and his heated eyes went to my slick pussy with his fingers buried deep inside me.

Pulling free, he coated my mouth with my essence and kissed me.

"Fucking, delicious," he hummed.

I reached between us, took hold of his thick, hard cock, positioned it at the opening of my aching sex, and slowly worked my way down. Each inch of him an exquisite treat to my senses.

"S-Sam," I gasped, my mission forgotten when his thumb returned to my oversensitive clit.

He gave me a wicked smile before he rolled me onto my back, coming over me.

"Now, Highness, we fuck."

Threading my fingers into his hair, I pulled him toward me. "Yes, now we fuck."

He pulled out and then rammed in, sinking hard and deep, just as I liked it. I wanted to feel it. I was small but not delicate.

He gave me exactly what I wanted, a fierce, no-holds-barred pounding, taking my breath and clouding my mind.

This need for his domination of me wasn't something I understood. This connection we shared was so intense, so emotional, so soul-consuming. It scared the hell out of me. And now, there was no severing it.

Who was I kidding? As he'd said, he etched himself into my heart and soul.

I clenched around him, the first tremors of an impending orgasm sneaking up on me.

"That's it. Come for me. Squeeze me tight."

I gasped and moaned, raked my nails down his back, and shattered. My pussy contracted and flexed, clamped down, and all my senses filled with utter bliss.

At the same time, Sam called out my name as he came, swirling his hips and pumping deep inside me.

MY HEART STILL THUNDERED IN MY CHEST WHEN SAM SAID, "If it wasn't clear already, I want the baby."

"I figured this out." I laughed and sobered as the reality of our situation crept in. "It makes one thing easier."

He remained quiet for a few moments and then asked, "Are you staying as primary on this assignment?"

I'd expected this question. But, pregnancy or not, I couldn't change the course of my plans. Too much rode on this.

"I have no choice. Everything revolves around me. Besides, I always see things through."

"Directors don't work in the field as you do. Most sit behind a desk."

"I'm not most."

He shifted, caging me with his arms. "Let someone else go in guns blazing."

"Sam, telling you doesn't change my plans. I'm seeing this through." I pushed him back, but he grabbed my wrist.

"You don't have to see everything through. Things are different now. You don't have to put yourself in danger."

Jerking my arm free, I stalked to my dress and picked it up.

"That is not your decision," I said as I searched for something to clean myself and saw my torn underwear.

Sam stood, bringing it to me. "Believe me, I know."

I took the silk from his fingers, wiped it between my legs, and then slipped on my gown.

Just as I reached for my zipper, Sam's fingers brushed mine. "I've got this."

I closed my eyes as the weight of this intimate act settled on my shoulders.

"Do you ever think of anything but your mission, goal, and people?" He stepped away, moved to his clothes, and dressed.

"You have no idea all the things I consider."

He clenched his jaw. "My baby is in there. Have you thought about that? What about me? Did you ever think about me in this grand mission of yours? I fucking love you. Do you even realize what it would feel like if anything happened to you?"

My temper flared, and without thinking, I shouted, "Who the fuck do you think I'm doing all of this for? It's for you. I'm giving you back your fucking legacy. I'm giving you the revenge you refuse to take. I'm going to make sure that monster pays for hurting every last one of you."

He stared at me, utter shock on his face. He clenched his jaw and closed his eyes for a brief second. Then, when he focused on me, a wave of anger like nothing he'd ever sent in my direction blasted toward me.

"Who told you I wanted any form of revenge on that bastard? Because it sure as hell wasn't me. What I told you I wanted was to watch him implode by his own doing."

"Sam—"

"No. I haven't finished. You created a multimillion-dollar operation to give me some revenge I never wanted. What good will Shah's death do for me? My mother is still gone."

A lump formed in the pit of my stomach, adding to the nausea continually churning there.

"If I ever get this legacy you are determined to give me, I will immediately give it to Jayna and Danika. It's tainted money, covered in my mother's blood." He pointed to me. "That baby in your belly is a King, not a fucking Shah. Our child will inherit Arin King's legacy. That man was my father, not Ashok Shah."

"Sam, I'm sorry. I was doing it because I—"

"You love me. Do you want to know what shows me that you love me? How about just using the fucking words and saying them to me? Just once, I'd like to hear you say it. Or perhaps shed this queen persona and come out in public with me. Let the world know you're my woman.

"You hate this life but wield it like a weapon. Something has to give, Devani. I won't compromise anymore. As of now, we are over in every aspect. I will be there for our child. I will do anything for our child. I meant it when I said, when it comes to us, I want it all or nothing."

18

SAM

I APPROACHED MY MOTHER'S GRAVEYARD A LITTLE BEFORE SIX in the morning. A deep heaviness settled into my chest, adding to everything else I held inside.

The scents of flowers and greenery filled the air. Groundskeepers busied themselves tending the area, ensuring every plot remained immaculately groomed.

I'd made sure of it.

Veda Milla Kumari never received the finer things during her young life. I would damn well make it so she had them while she lay in rest.

When Arin took us in, he'd offered to have her cremated since no one was there upon her death to explain the traditions of my mother's faith and culture. I'd been too young to have a say, and honestly, my grief had consumed me.

In the end, I'd decided to leave her in the cemetery. She'd already spent years here. I couldn't disturb her peace.

She deserved it more than anyone I knew.

Kneeling, I set a bouquet of irises and roses at the base of her headstone. Slowly, I traced her name and the two dates carved into the marble.

Almost twenty-seven years apart, exactly.

The day my world had turned upside down, Mum and I had planned to celebrate her birthday early since her factory scheduled her to work a double shift on the actual date.

We had everything planned. I'd go to school with the neighbor's daughter while she met with coworkers for breakfast and went to a quick business meeting. Then, after she picked me up from school, we would go for pizza at our favorite place in the neighborhood.

Our grand plan never came to fruition. Instead, a social worker had shown up at my school to ask me if I had any known family. There were none. None that had ever attempted to know me, anyway.

Mum's family wasn't wealthy by Shah's standards but was well-respected in the Indo-American community. Having an unwed and pregnant daughter would have shamed them and ruined the marriage prospects for the other three children in their family. My maternal grandparents chose their standing in society over their child and grandchild.

I wanted to hate them for what they'd done to Mum, but what I felt toward them was indifference. They'd locked themselves up in tradition and lost out. Arin had taken great pleasure in showing them what I'd become.

To me, it meant nothing. I would rather have had my mother.

"Jai Shri Krishna, Mum. I'm sorry it took me a while to visit," I said in Gujarati. *"I know for a fact that Shah killed you."* I retraced her name. *"But, I'm sure you already knew this."*

I paused as if she'd respond.

After analyzing all of the images on Kala Barot's phone, disgust like nothing I'd ever felt settled in my stomach. When Arin had spoken to me about the accident, I knew deep down Shah had orchestrated the bus crash. But not the role he'd played.

By tampering with the bus, he'd covered his hands in the blood of Mum, Nik's, Kir's, and Rey's parents, and eight other innocent people.

"I've finally put all the pieces together of what happened that morning. You were going to meet with Shah's parents and tell them about me. That was why you agreed to go to breakfast with your coworkers and got on the bus."

I pulled a few flowers from the bouquet and set them around the base of the headstone.

"There is so much more that I've learned. I'm still wrapping my mind around it. I'm sure you know all of this too. How do I accept this when I don't even like the guy?"

I could almost hear her say, *"Because he's family and had as little choice in this as you did."*

"One last thing before I go. This one is a big one." I released a deep breath. *"You're going to be a grandmother. It definitely wasn't planned. I guess you are the one person who would understand. I'm not sure how things will go with Devani. We are in a battle of wills."*

I scrubbed a hand down my face.

"She set up her whole operation to give me this revenge I never wanted. Killing him won't bring you back. I'd rather keep him alive and watch every little thing he built tumble around him because of his greed. Then, when he tries to pick up the pieces, be the one to remind him of all he lost by taking that from him too."

I dropped my head as realization dawned on me. Everything I'd said to Devani was complete bullshit.

I may have put the idea of killing Shah to the side but not the notion of destroying him.

Initially, it had been a game of sorts. I'd felt a slight sense of satisfaction every time I made money for King Holdings and took a deal, a property, a position on a board, anything, even something inconsequential from Shah or his partners.

If I was truly going to lay it out there for myself, revenge laced every fucking thing I'd done. Especially after Shah had orchestrated Kir's accident and Jayna's stabbing.

I'd catered to my ruthless reputation. Shah couldn't move without feeling my presence, from the support I'd given Monica Shah during their divorce to the donations I'd made to help his opponent win during Shah's bid for the Senate.

Arin wanted revenge for me all those years ago, and I'd never realized it. Or I'd pretended not to understand it.

"Let Ashok Shah see the son he threw away sitting as a king on a throne while he lingers below."

Arin knew I had to channel my anger, and he'd given me an outlet. One that had helped make the family filthy rich. I'd never be able to figure out how he knew what to do with each of us.

I released a deep breath and skimmed a palm across the grass near my feet.

"Well, Mum. It looks like I lied to her. She saw it, and I didn't. I know what you'd say. I better fix it. Not sure how that is going to happen. From the information I've gotten, she has to see this mission through. She's in danger, and it's killing me to know I can't do anything to help her."

"Are you so sure about that?" A question came in Gujarati from behind me.

In a flash, I pivoted, pulling my pistol from the back of my pants. My security team followed suit and positioned themselves next to me, ready to protect me if necessary.

I stared directly into Neil Joshi's eyes.

He held my gaze, unconcerned by the multitude of weapons pointed at him, and behind him stood that fucker, Noah Carter.

I remembered Carter from the time Lilly worked with Solon. The asshole had pretended to be some British earl or some bullshit back then when in reality, he was a Colorado rancher.

I remained quiet, studying Neil.

We'd never met formally, and the few times he'd passed me, outside of pegging him for a cop, I kept my focus on Devani. But, now that he stood before me, I couldn't deny the truth.

We shared almost the same height and build. Even our eyes looked the same. Well, outside of the color, with Neil's being a deep brown with a bit of gold and mine the exact shade of Shah's, amber. Then there was the jawline we'd both gotten from the bastard.

Neil narrowed his eyes and clenched his jaw.

He knew I knew.

"Do you want to help her, King?" The edge in his tone made it very clear that the other subject wasn't open for discussion.

"My answer depends on the conditions."

"It's simple. You help me complete my objective for this assignment, and I will make sure you get your queen."

I smirked. "No one can make sure my queen does anything. That is the issue at hand. She is singular when it comes to her missions."

"You're willing to let her risk your child?"

"So you know?"

"She told us. We're her family." The possessiveness in Neil's voice gave me the urge to punch him. "Returning to my previous question, will you let Devani continue to put herself in danger?"

"No one lets Devani do anything. She won't stop until the very end if she knew the information I do."

"What do you think you know?"

I lowered my gun, with only half of my men standing down. The others remained on guard and ready to shoot.

"I know enough that if you saw the list I did, you would put a bullet in your father's head within seconds of seeing him next."

Neil gave no reaction outside of the rage whirling inside his irises.

After a few moments, he said, "He's not my father, but you already knew this. And his time on this earth lasts as long as he is useful."

"Before we go any further, let me make something clear." I holstered my firearm and adjusted my coat. "Devani is what matters to me. I don't give a shit about your mission or your fucking objective. I'm not Solon. However, if you fail to take the Circle of Ten down, my brothers and I will do everything in our power to eliminate them and their network."

"Why are you after them?"

"Let's just say they tried to erase the existence of a little boy after his mother's death."

"I see. So this runs on the side of elimination versus retribution."

"You should know, our tactics aren't instantaneous. Instead, we like to draw things out and make them public. This way, our prey wishes it was pure elimination."

"Thanks for the warning, King. I plan to take care of them and won't need you to clean up any mess."

"Then why ask for my help?"

"It isn't for me. It's for Van. Her pregnancy puts her at risk, and she doesn't even know it."

"I'm listening."

"First, I need your agreement."

"She's mine. That's all the answer you need."

"That's a bit possessive for a man who walked away from her."

Instead of giving him any outward indication that his dig struck home, I asked, "Was that a question?"

"In the fifteen years I've known her, she's never let any man twist her up the way you have. Now I believe I've figured out what it is about you she finds so irresistible." He smirked. "You're both assholes. Like attracts like."

I almost commented on him being as much of an asshole as me since we were related, but I kept that to myself. I doubted he'd have found any humor in my words, especially knowing the method of his conception and the horrors his mother had endured.

I'd accepted Nik, Kir, and Rey as my brothers without sharing blood. When I'd learned about Jayna, it hadn't mattered her mom was the one to replace mine. Jayna was still my sister, and not once had I felt anything but compassion for Monica Shah. Through no fault of her own, she'd become a victim of a fucked-up circumstance.

"I am an asshole. I own it. If you want my assistance, I get a favor to call in at a time and place of my choosing."

"Your assistance will more than likely save the lives of your unborn child and their mother. So I would say it is a net even collaboration."

"Don't give me that bullshit. I know what great lengths you go to protect your agents. The multimillion-dollar operation Carter and his European team implemented to save Lilly is proof enough. Meet my terms, and you have a deal."

"What is it you think I want you to help me do?"

"You want me to follow through with my original plan and destroy Joshi, Shah, and the remaining Circle of Ten. You want me to do it in the most public way possible while keeping your mother and sister squeaky clean. And while I'm doing my part, you will eliminate everyone who fucked with your mother and sister."

"What makes you believe that's my goal?"

"Call it deductive reasoning."

Joshi's jaw clenched. Fucker thought he could get to me with the walking away dig. I knew all about how much his mother and sister meant to him. I understood his need to protect them.

I'd crush anyone who dared touch Jayna or Danika.

"It looks like you fell into a vault of information about me, King."

"I make it my business to acquire knowledge about everyone. Now back to the previous topic. You want my help. I want a favor to call in at my time and place of choosing."

"Within reason."

"There is no reasoning with Kings. You should know this. We take what you offer and expect more. Do we have a deal, Joshi?"

Neil sighed and then nodded. "Deal. With two manipulative assholes for parents, I hope your kid makes your life hell."

"Now that we've finished the negotiation part of the evening, get to the real reason you need my help. Why is she a target? What makes her so valuable pregnant?"

Solon agents were trained to string things into long-winded conversations where they gave just enough information to get what they needed out of a deal without compromising their mission. I'd spent nearly three years sparring with the master of those games. It was the only reason I'd insisted on the favor bargain in the first place. I'd used it to gauge big brother's intent and learn a few things about him.

Chief among them, his hatred for Joshi and Shah surpassed mine.

I waited for Neil to respond to my question, but when he spoke, it took all my strength not to punch him in the face.

"She's carrying Ashok Shah's legacy."

"The fuck she is," I shouted.

My men immediately shifted, and Noah, who'd remained almost out of sight, moved in beside Neil, ready to intervene.

On the other hand, Neil remained still, not a flinch or a slight shift in muscle.

Complete control.

Then as if I wasn't ready to kill him, he asked, "Want to know what makes the Joshi-Shah friendship so great?"

"I'm sure you're going to tell me."

"Nothing. They despise each other. But they created this business tying them together." Now the hatred he felt for the men showed through in his eyes. "It's a business based on creating legacies for the affluent. The second he learns Devani is pregnant, he will find some way to lay claim to that child."

"He can't claim another man's child."

"Shah's made it well known that he and his new wife are trying for a child. This baby has everything he covets— his bloodline and the right pedigree. Do you honestly think he won't take extreme measures to ensure he gets what he wants?"

"I will kill him with my bare hands if he touches her."

"That would require you to be with her, and you're not."

Brother or not, this fucker had ten seconds before I punched him in the face.

"You came here for a purpose, Joshi. Enough with the usual Solon bullshit. Get to your point."

"You're going to fix things with Devani and take her out of play."

"You've lost your mind if you believe I have any sway regarding her work."

Neil lifted a brow. "You cracked the queen's shell. You have more power than you know."

"Does she know you're going behind her back?"

"Feel free to tell her. I've made my position on this situation clear. But as usual, she values herself less than others."

I narrowed my gaze as a surge of jealousy hit me. Neil held a bond with Devani built over experiences I could never touch.

"You love her?"

"Yes." He waited, letting that one word hang in the air.

The glint in his eyes made it clear he'd paused to fuck with me.

Asshole.

Then, he smirked and continued. "As a sister. She's too much a diva for my tastes."

"Good thing she's not yours."

"But is she yours?"

"Why is it so important I make things right with her?"

"So she is out of the way when I take the revenge she planned to give you, little brother."

19

DEVANI

A LITTLE BEFORE EIGHT IN THE EVENING, I WORKED MY WAY through the underground tunnel leading into the interior of the Dayal-King Gallery.

I'd expected a summons from Danika, correction, the Little Rabbit weeks ago, and it surprised me she'd waited this long. When Danika wanted answers, she went to great lengths to acquire them.

I couldn't fault her. Her whole life revolved around information, being a hacker and all.

Pushing a loose panel to the side, I stepped into the appraisal section of the gallery.

Behind a large workstation, Danika leaned back in her chair as she rubbed the swell of her belly. I had no doubt she'd known the second I'd stepped within fifty feet of her building. And she'd activated the security system as soon as I crawled into my usual access point.

Sometimes, I hated being so predictable.

Her hazel eyes met mine, and she asked, "Do you remember when I told you not so long ago that it would happen to you?"

"I require specifics, then maybe I'll understand your meaning." I moved toward her and then cocked a hip against her desk.

"Oh, I'm going to explain in great detail."

I pursed my lips. "Let me hear it."

"It was always more than you wanted us to believe. I know the reason why you kept pushing Sam away and why you couldn't let him go."

"I'm sure you're going to tell me."

"Sam broke through that rock-hard shell of yours, and you melted the ice in his veins."

Her words seared as if she'd struck a fiery poker deep into my gut. It only added to the crushing pain that refused to ease ever since Sam walked out of the theater dressing room a week ago.

Keeping my face void of emotion, I asked in the bitchy voice everyone accepted as part of my personality, "Is there a point to this?"

"He's your weakness. And a Solon agent can't have a weakness, especially not a director. Am I correct, Director Patel?" Danika matched my snark.

Bitch never let me get away with anything.

"Did you call me here to gloat?"

"I made you come here because you need to call in that favor I owe you."

"What favor?"

"You know exactly the one I'm talking about." She glared at me.

Oh, I knew. A few years ago, Ashok Shah had planned to use video surveillance footage to frame Nik for Kir's murder. Although only a handful of people knew at the time, Kir had survived the wreck. My team and I eliminated any trace of Nik's involvement in the cleanup following Kir's near-fatal car accident.

"I've got it covered."

"Is it so fucking hard for you to depend on others, Devani? You don't have to do everything alone."

I sighed. "It isn't that, I promise. You technically are my backup plan. Well, you and Lilly."

"Since when the hell am I a backup plan? I'm the fucking nuclear option." She sat up, outrage on her face. "Do you know what's at stake?"

"I know exactly what's at stake. It's all I've thought about. I'm stubborn, Dani. Not stupid."

She shifted her chair to face me fully. "I want to hear it all."

"You're pretty bossy when riled up, shorty."

"Fuck off. You're only an inch and a half taller than me. Now get to it."

I couldn't help but laugh as I pushed onto the edge of her desk.

Once seated, I said, "I'm going to fuck this case up

royally. The plan is to take it to such a level of bad that there isn't any recovery from it. As a result, I may have to retire from the organization altogether."

The scowl on her face made it very clear she found nothing amusing in my words. More than likely, she'd give it her best shot to tie me to a chair to keep me in place if she hated what I told her next.

I glanced down at the platinum cuff on my wrist and then traced the names written in Sanskrit hidden among intricate patterns etched into the metal.

I'd known what it meant when Sam had given me the gift, even if I'd refused to admit it.

That was probably the day we'd passed the point of no return.

"You were already planning to retire, so keep going before I lose my shit."

I returned my focus to Danika's striking face and stated, "The Queen of Diamonds is going to claim her King."

"SO YOU'RE GOING TO DO THIS?" NEIL'S VOICE CAME through the transmitter attached to the back of my earring as I cleared the last security checkpoints to enter the Carina Hotel.

"Absolutely."

"You could have given me a little warning."

"You're on the line with me now."

This evening, all of New York's elite had gathered for a charity casino night hosted by the King brothers. Anyone who garnered an invitation would attend without question, including Ashok Shah and all he considered his societal group of friends and acquaintances.

I understood why the Kings allowed their enemies admission to their events. They enjoyed playing with their prey.

However, when my invitation arrived, personally addressed by Sam, I wasn't sure if he requested my presence as a guest or as an adversary to watch.

In the end, it hadn't mattered. I'd already planned to crash the party, whether invited or not.

"There are too many unknowns, Devani," Neil said. "I would have come with you. Instead, you're breaking all protocols."

"Bringing you is counterproductive to my objective."

"That's not what I meant, and you know it. You're in danger."

"I don't scare easily. Didn't you learn that lesson earlier today at the facility?"

When Neil told me what he'd suspected about Shah's plans for me, my temper had boiled to the point of exploding.

It had taken a great deal of self-control not to go over to Shah's mansion and send the fucker to the afterlife.

Pregnancy may have fucked with my emotions and zapped my energy, but it in no way made me weak or unable to defend myself. On the contrary, I trained daily with only minor modifications recommended by my physician. I still had no problem taking men bigger than Neil down when necessary.

"Yes, yes. You laugh in the face of danger. I hope King knows what he's in for."

"He knows. I've knocked him onto his back plenty of times too."

A wave of uncertainty flowed through me for a moment before I pushed it away. No, I wouldn't let anything mess with my concentration. Too much depended on tonight.

I squared my shoulders and then glided a hand down the front of the gown, lingering for a moment on my once flat stomach before smoothing out one of my dress pleats.

As I approached the doors to the ballroom, I noticed Ashok Shah leaning against a high-top table. He studied me with a bit too much interest. His wife chatted with a group of socialites, completely oblivious her husband's attention was anywhere but on her. However, the expression on his face as he watched me gave me the urge to punch him.

"Shah's in the vicinity. Going quiet," I warned Neil.

I took a glass of water from a passing server and moved in Shah's direction.

"Hello. How are you tonight?"

"I'm fine." He glanced behind me. "Where's Neil?"

"At home."

"You came without him?" He asked the question as if my presence alone disturbed him.

"Yes." I sipped my water, letting the cool liquid soothe my parched throat. "We aren't attached at the hip."

"He doesn't have an issue with you associating with the Kings?"

"I don't need permission from him or anyone to do anything." Inhaling to calm my irritation, I allowed my Queen of Diamonds mask to settle over me.

It looked as if the bitchy side of my persona needed to make an appearance before I could get down to business this evening.

"You don't want your reputation tarnished by the company you keep."

I narrowed my gaze, tilting my chin slightly. "Then, we should say goodbye."

Surprise flashed on his face as the dig settled in. During all the time of our association, I'd kept a calm and cordial demeanor, but now the gloves were off.

"Well, Devani. Before you run off, I have something to say to you." His chiding tone made it seem as if he were a father about to reprimand a child.

I would have walked away from the pompous ass. However, curiosity had me waiting for Shah to speak.

"You will marry Neil within the next month. Is that clear?"

"Motherfucker," I heard Neil mutter into my transmitter. "Keep him talking, and don't let him rile you."

I knew how to do my job. Of course, I technically wasn't on the job tonight, but all the best-laid plans and all that.

"Excuse me?" I asked, cocking a hand on my hip as I set my glass on the tray of a passing server. "I do not take orders from anyone. Least of all you."

"Let me make this clear. You will marry the father of my grandchild."

How could he know about the pregnancy?

"Excuse me. Neil is Arun Joshi's child."

Ashok laughed. "The only place that man is his father is on paper. All I need to do is shave this beard, and everyone will see it. Neil looks identical to the way I did in my youth."

Was he bragging?

I kept my tone as cold as ice when I said, "Except the eyes, you mean. Those went to Sam."

If he wanted to put all of his deeds out on the table, I'd oblige.

Rage washed over his face, then just as fast, he schooled it away. We were in a public venue, after all.

"You will marry Neil."

"What makes you believe you have power over me?"

"I know more secrets about your family than you can ever believe. The only way you'll keep your family's reputation pure is by ensuring my grandchild won't come into the world a bastard."

"First of all, I don't give two shits about my family or its reputation. I told my uncles this when they threatened me with a similar thing. So I'll respond in the same fashion to you." I leaned forward, staring into his eyes. "Burn it all to hell."

Standing straight again, I said, "Now to the second part of your declaration. What makes you so sure that I'm expecting?"

"The Queen of Diamonds is never without a cocktail or coffee. You've given up both."

"Did you ever think I may have changed my diet due to all the parties I've attended lately? I'm also known for liking cake. I haven't given that up." I shifted, turning in the direction of the ballroom. "I believe I'll go play some poker now."

As I took my first step, he asked, "Are you saying you aren't pregnant with Neil's child?"

Pausing midstep, I took a breath. At the same time, my eyes connected with Sam's amber ones on the far side of the ballroom. My body immediately reacted, wanting him, needing him. His gaze penetrated me as if he saw into my soul.

"No, I'm not pregnant with Neil's child."

"But, you are pregnant?" Shah questioned.

My heartbeat accelerated, and I licked my lips. Here I went.

"I am."

"Who's the father?" Anger radiated out of every word.

I couldn't help but smile and answered over my shoulder, "Samir King."

After taking a few steps into the ballroom, Neil spoke into my earpiece. "No going back now."

"Nope," I whispered, then added, "I'm sorry, Neil."

"It is what it is. It isn't about me tonight. In the end, you may have just done us a favor and accelerated things."

"I'm going eliminate him for both of you," I promised.

"Oh no. You don't get to take this from me. We had an agreement. That fucker is all mine now. Enjoy your evening, Director. Signing off."

The line went dead.

I reached up to tuck my hair behind my ear and simultaneously removed the communication piece.

Work no longer mattered. I had other plans. Sliding the equipment into my clutch, I weaved through the crowd.

Sam sat with the rest of the Kings in the center of the room. Each brother hosted a table with their wife. Sam, who had an empty chair next to him, was the exception.

Had he expected me, or was it for someone else?

Then I caught a smirk on Danika's lips and knew she'd arranged it.

I hadn't given her a single detail of my plan at the gallery. And I'd waited until a few hours ago to accept Sam's invitation.

How she'd guessed I would show up tonight, I'd never know. Then again, Wonder Girl knew things others only dreamed of learning.

Sam shifted in his seat, directing his attention entirely on me as that familiar pulse of energy surged between us.

Heat filled his amber irises, as did that one emotion I tried so hard to ignore for far too long.

Love.

My heartbeat drummed in my ears, and my stomach

fluttered with nerves like nothing I'd ever experienced in my life.

The weight of attention I garnered as I moved through the room and toward Sam sat heavily on my shoulders. I'd spent my life in the spotlight, and scrutiny never bothered me.

Except tonight, I felt as if I had everything on the line.

I held Sam's hypnotizing stare until I reached the back of the empty seat at his table.

"Mr. King, is there room for another player to join your game?"

Sam scanned me exactly as he'd done all those years ago. He assessed everything about me—my face, my clothes, my jewelry. His pupils dilated and heated, turning his irises into rings of gold as they lingered on my wrist and ears.

"Of course." He took a sip of his drink and then gestured to the vacant seat. "However, I should warn you. We've entered the high-stakes portion of the evening. Buy-ins are steep."

"I'm sure you know I can cover any bet level." Sliding into the chair next to him, I shifted, letting the side of my leg brush against his.

"At this table, the stakes aren't monetary."

"I see. And what exactly are we playing for?"

"We work in favors and such. What can you offer in that realm?"

"Well, that's complicated."

"I can navigate complicated."

"What I have to offer is of great value, especially to the Kings. One in particular."

Something flashed over his face. I wasn't sure if it was shock or longing. Then, just as fast, it disappeared.

"Go on."

Taking a deep breath, I knew it was now or never.

I reached forward, took the tumbler from his hand, and immediately he grabbed my wrist, blocking my movement.

The table suddenly grew quiet, giving me the exact reaction I'd expected.

Many people in this room were regular patrons of The Library. They knew Sam and I were beyond acquaintances. The rules of The Library stated that what anyone saw or heard there never left the club. And when I'd walked out of a room with him, no one said a word.

I had no doubt seeing me in public with Sam surprised the hell out of them and made them realize we were a lot more than casual.

Plus, members of the media sat throughout the room, taking in the scene. Even if they couldn't hear the conversation about to happen between a King brother and the notorious Queen of Diamonds, they'd report we were together.

"What are you doing?" He leaned forward and then said, in a reprimanding tone that had me holding in a smirk, "You can't drink."

"What makes you believe I ever planned to indulge?" I licked my lips and watched his golden gaze drift down for a brief second. "Maybe I wanted your undivided attention."

"Well, now you have it." He brought my hand down, taking the tumbler of whiskey from my fingers and replacing it with a glass of water. "Including the other players at the table and most of this ballroom."

I ignored the weight of his warning. Our future depended on this. However, the people at the table or around us had no need to hear the extent of our conversation.

I shifted closer to him, my knees sandwiched between his and my face too close for mere strangers. I wasn't even sure if he realized it, but he'd set a possessive palm on my hip, in plain sight of everyone.

"You asked me what I could offer as an alternative to my money. Don't you want to hear my answer?"

"You said it was for the Kings. There is only one King at this table. What makes you think I'll win to take it?"

"I suspect knowing what's at stake will incentivize the win."

"Now I'm intrigued. What is it you're offering?"

"Me and your future heir growing inside me."

He swallowed, his fingers flexing against my hip as a war of emotions played out in his amber eyes. "Be sure what you're saying. There is no going back."

"Sam, I'm here in a room full of media and New York society. You're holding me. I'm saying I love you, that I belong with you."

When he remained silent, just staring at me, I added, "Do I qualify to play at this table?"

He shook his head. "What you're offering is beyond anything anyone at this table can match."

"Then perhaps a private game?" I picked up my glass, drank down my water, then spoke the words I'd used after I challenged him to that first game. "That is, unless you're afraid to lose to a queen."

His lips curved, and he offered me his hand. "A King never steps away from a challenge, especially from a queen."

I slid my palm over his. Immediately, his heat seeped into my skin, soothing the ache deep in my chest.

We both rose together, that energy between us crackling like usual.

"Lead the way, Mr. King."

20

SAM

I WRAPPED MY ARM AROUND DEVANI'S WAIST, AWARE OF THE stares we garnered.

When I'd sent her the invitation, I never expected her to accept or to arrive at my table the way she had.

In fact, I'd planned to visit her penthouse later this evening.

After all the revelations of the last few weeks, I'd reevaluated my stance on several things in my life—chief among them, the succession of the trust left by my paternal grandmother to her grandchildren. The trust stated that the eldest grandchild inherited Shah International. I wasn't the eldest. Therefore, I had no problem letting every penny of it go to the rightful heir.

I glanced down at Devani as we moved around tables

and through the crowd of gala attendees. She wore an understated black gown that should have looked simple considering the attire of the other guests but instead drew attention to her. And she'd repeated her jewelry choice from the night at The Library, wearing only the earrings I'd given her and the cuff on her wrist.

As always, the Queen of Diamonds was never predictable.

After three years, she'd finally decided and announced it in the most public fashion imaginable.

"So that you know," I said to her, "if you hadn't shown up, I would have found you."

A smile touched her lips. "Good thing I got to you first."

We made our way to the front of the hotel, where my driver waited with the limo.

The second the doors closed, we reached for each other. Our lips and hands were desperate to touch and taste.

Her mouth was so sweet and intoxicating. We warred for dominance while needing to savor as well as devour and claim.

She pushed at my tux jacket as I glided my palms over the curves of her hips, along her waist, and up to her beautiful heavy breasts, cupping them, molding them.

Fuck, they were perfect.

"Sam," she moaned as I pinched her sensitive nipples through her dress. "I ache for you."

Her words sent a primal shot of lust straight to my

cock, making it go rock hard. I fisted her hair, breaking our kiss, and jerked her head back.

I grazed my teeth over her lower lip, giving her a slight sting. "You're mine now, Highness. You're in my world now. There is no escape for you."

Before I realized her intent, she jerked her hips and simultaneously shoved my shoulders, flipping me over and pinning my back to the bench seat of the limo.

"I believe you have that wrong." She loomed over me. "It is more like you're the prisoner of a queen, and it's a life sentence."

I stared into her dark eyes. The impact of her words sat heavily between us.

I'd spent my life learning to rein in my emotion and build an impenetrable wall around my heart. Then with sheer will, she'd shattered my defenses.

"Sam, I mean it." She leaned down, cupping my jaw. "You said you wanted it all. That's what I'm offering."

I sat up, bringing her with me. "Are you fine with giving up your position in society?"

"I'm not giving up anything. I'm retiring." She lifted a brow as her full lips curved at the corners.

She knew damn well I wasn't asking about Solon. Plus, the possibility of Devani leaving the organization one hundred percent erred on par with pigs sprouting wings and flying.

"I don't want you to have doubts."

"No doubts. I planned to walk away regardless."

The meaning behind her words hit me like a ton of

bricks. She planned to leave everything behind, not just the agency—retirement in all senses.

"When did you make this decision?"

"When I set up the case." Her face fell for a brief second. "Sam, you were right. I didn't ask you what you wanted."

"No, I was wrong for the shit I said. You saw my actions against Shah and took those as cues for what I wanted."

A frown marred her brow. "I'm not following."

I closed my eyes, released a breath, and then laid it all out. "I've spent my whole life plotting Shah's fall. I wanted him to suffer for taking my mother from me and my brothers' parents from them. His death would never have given me the peace I wanted. Watching as he lost everything was the sweetest form of revenge."

"So, in other words, we're dumbasses that need to stop doing things on our own and work together."

"Something like that." I smiled. "One other thing."

"Go on."

"As I said, I don't want a dime of the billion-dollar Shah inheritance. Besides, I have no claim to it. I'm not the oldest Shah grandchild. I'd rather make sure the rightful heir gets everything."

"Neil," she whispered.

I nodded. "Never thought I'd say this, but he deserves Shah's head on a platter more than anyone I know."

"There isn't a scale of comparison, Sam. What each of you experienced made you into the men you are today."

The limo stopped outside Devani's high-rise. Paparazzi lined various spots along the walkways and sides of the building as a multitude of security staff guarded the pathway leading to the doors.

"Looks like news of our grand exit from the hotel has circulated to the masses."

"You would have told your driver to take us to your place if you truly wanted to avoid the attention."

Cupping her face, I ran a thumb over her lower lip. "Ready for the public to know you're mine?"

"Since we're arriving at my place, wouldn't I be the one making a claim?"

"By all means, Highness. I've waited three years for this."

I knocked on the window, indicating to one of my security detail that he could open the door.

The next ten minutes went in a blur of flashes, shouts, and maneuvering through a crowd of reporters. I'd generally kept a low profile regarding societal news, and spectacles on this level were rare.

Now with the Queen of Diamonds as my lady, I had a feeling all that was a thing of the past.

The second we stepped into Devani's private elevator, she asked with a smirk, "Rethinking our relationship, Mr. King?"

"Not a chance." I crowded her back against the wall of the cab. "Plus, you should know, once a King accepts terms, there's no getting out of them."

She skimmed a palm up my chest and grasped the lapel of my tuxedo jacket. "Good to know."

We held each other's stares as the elevator chimed and

opened into the foyer of Devani's penthouse.

"Well, Mr. King. Would you like to come in through the front door of my home?"

I smiled down at her. "Absolutely."

In the next second, she pulled me toward her, sealing our mouths together. I lifted her into my arms and walked her into the apartment.

Her clutch fell to the floor as she threaded her fingers into my hair and wrapped her legs around my waist. Somehow, we stumbled to her bedroom, losing her heels along the way.

When I set her on her feet, she gazed up at me with utterly unguarded desire-clouded eyes.

"Stop staring at me like that and do something," she ordered.

Instead of saying anything, I grabbed the shoulders of her gown and ripped the material from her body, leaving her clad only in her black lace bustier set and thigh-high stockings.

She pursed her lips as if she held in a knowing smile.

"You knew what you were getting when you picked me."

"I did." Turning, she lifted her hair and offered me her back. "This may not be as easy to discard. I suggest using the fastenings and zipper."

With slow, precise movements, I removed her corset and skimmed my lips up the soft skin along her spine and shoulders. Once finished, I fisted her hair, tilted her head back, and took her mouth again in a searing kiss.

I slid my palm over the slight curve of her stomach, chest, and up to her throat, giving her the slight squeeze she craved so much.

A low moan escaped her lips, and goose bumps prickled her skin.

I savored her taste, loving every bit of her. She filled my senses. Her fingers flexed against my thighs, kneading the material of my pants.

She turned in my arms, suddenly becoming the aggressor and pushing at my clothes. "I want you naked."

"I have no issues with this." I shrugged my jacket off my shoulders as she untied my bowtie, and within minutes, I stood before her divested of all clothing.

Her heated gaze raked me from head to toe, lingering longer than necessary on my cock.

"Devani," I warned.

Without shifting focus, she licked her lips and answered, "Yes."

My control snapped, and I pulled her toward me.

"About fucking time." She bit my lower lip, just shy of too hard.

I growled and tugged her head back, meeting her viciousness with my own by scoring my teeth along the column of her neck.

"Always manipulating." I slid my palms down her body, molding her curves.

"I—I have a reputation for a reason."

"That you do." I cupped and pinched her nipples,

eliciting a whimper from her lips. "You could try the direct approach. You may get a better response."

Her eyes narrowed as she brought her body flush with mine.

"How's this for direct? Fuck me raw and dirty, Mr. King. I dare you."

I grasped her jaw, lowering my face to hers. "I hear your challenge. However, I have a counteroffer."

"And that is?"

"I dare you to let yourself go. Let yourself feel. Let yourself be vulnerable. There is nothing wrong with gentle, soft, and emotional."

Her lips trembled. "Sam."

"Let me cherish you, Highness."

She nodded her head as a tear slipped down her cheek. "Okay."

Thumbing the wetness off her face, I leaned forward and grazed my mouth over hers in slow passes, coaxing, teasing. She shivered, fluttering her eyes closed and releasing a low sigh from her lips.

I lifted her into my arms, carried her to the bed, and laid her upon the plush duvet, caging her with my body.

"Do you even know how beautiful you are?"

She smirked. "I'm well aware of my looks. I know what I see in the mirror."

"I'm not talking about your face. I mean the woman in here." I set my hand over her heart. "You care more than anyone I have ever met, and you'll put everything on the line just to protect others, even if it means sacrificing yourself."

She glanced away for a brief moment, revealing a shyness she rarely showed anyone.

"Don't make me something I'm not. I'm far from a saint."

"Oh no, you're no saint. More of an avenging angel."

"Fallen angel is more like it." The features of her face softened, and she reached up and cupped my face, running her fingers over the stubble on my chin before threading them into the hair at the back of my head. "Then, you'll have to accept you're no different than I am."

I dropped my forehead to hers. "I have no problem admitting the truth."

"And that is?"

"I will burn the world down for those I love." I held her gaze. "Can you guess who most of all?"

"I love you, Sam." She brought her lips a fraction from mine. "I'm an assassin. There isn't anything I won't do if someone fucked with the man I love."

The way she spoke those words, without hesitation, given so freely, filled a wound in my heart I hadn't realized still festered. For years, I'd waited, wanted. She'd refused to say it and kept me from uttering the words.

As if sensing my thoughts, she whispered, "I'm sorry I waited so long to tell you. I should have said it sooner."

"At least, you finally caught up."

"What can I say? I'm stubborn, not stupid." She brought

her mouth flush against mine and said, "Will you make love to me, Sam?"

"With pleasure."

We spoke no more words, letting our mouths, hands, and bodies taste, touch, and feel on a level we hadn't allowed ourselves to go before.

When I slid into her, there was no hard fucking but a slow, intimate exploration and memorization of every gasp, moan, and sigh. Just as our orgasms shattered over us, we held each other's gazes knowing no barriers would stand between us again.

———

"A SK ME. I KNOW YOU'RE DYING TO. SO GET IT OUT," DEVANI ordered as she adjusted herself against me.

We'd spent the better part of the night lost in each other and maybe slept three hours. Now the sunrise peeked over the distant skyscrapers, illuminating the bedroom in a wash of golden light, and we had to clear up a few more things.

"What happened to seeing this case through until the very end?"

"I'm still seeing it through, just in a different capacity. Neil is primary now."

"Want to elaborate?"

"When I left with you last night, I changed the course of this mission. I either fucked up the case royally or accelerated the end."

"Meaning, you made yourself a bigger target." I leaned over her, brushing the hair back from her forehead. "You're the prize for the beloved son, and I stole you."

"I'm the compromised prize. Shah would never want me for his son, and neither would Joshi."

"Exactly how are you compromised, outside of being with me?"

"I told Shah I'm pregnant with your child."

I stared at her, not sure I'd heard her correctly. "Let me get this straight. Last night, in addition to announcing our relationship to New York society, you revealed to Shah that you're carrying my child?"

"It wasn't as if I intended to say anything, but he ordered me to marry Neil. He assumed my lack of caffeine and alcohol intake meant I was pregnant with his grandchild. I had to correct his error."

Shah wasn't even close to a grandfather to my child.

"You could have just denied it."

A part of me wished she had, for her sake, her safety. She had no idea what she'd done by revealing this to him.

She shook her head. "No more lies when it comes to us. I told you, I'm all in."

"It's not that." I cupped her face. "You're in more danger than you've ever been before."

"I highly doubt it." She snorted and then offered me her hand. "Hi, I'm Van, Director of Solon North America. By the time I turned fifteen, many considered me a deadly weapon. And on my first assignment, I went into a war zone to assassinate a general."

I could have gone my whole life without knowing that bit of information.

My kid was never following in their mother's footsteps.

"You're not understanding, Devani. Shah has lost everything to the Kings. Danika, Jayna, the majority of his fortune, and now you. You're carrying the one thing he wants more than anything on earth."

Realization entered her dark eyes. "A legacy. An heir."

"He can never claim Neil as his son without revealing the circumstances of his birth. And no matter how much Arun Joshi despises Neil, he'll never relinquish his claim on him."

"I'm not now nor ever have been someone to keep under lock and key. So don't get any ideas." She narrowed her gaze, almost in a calculating fashion. "And don't think to put a tail on me. Slipping that shit is something I can do in my sleep."

"I'm not an idiot. I couldn't cage you even if I tried."

"Glad we established this before our relationship moved to the next level."

"Enough with channeling Danika." I sighed and dropped my forehead against hers. "Shah hates me. I've spent my life taking from him. Don't you think he will find some way to hurt you to keep me from having the one thing he'll never get?"

The vision of Jayna lying in her hospital bed, wrapped in grief from losing her child after her attack, filled my mind. And then I thought of Kir's mangled body following the wreck, barely recognizable. Two people I'd nearly lost because of Shah's hatred.

Devani cupped my face with both her hands. "Sam, I'm not like most people. I can protect myself."

"It may not be enough. This isn't about strength or skill. You threw down the gauntlet yesterday."

"I feel as if I'm missing something."

"That's because you are. I agreed to buy out all of Neil's shares in Joshi International, including his voting rights for Shah International." I stared into her eyes. "The deal was executed yesterday at noon. Then I put everything into a trust for Mia Joshi with you as the executor of said trust."

"Well, that complicates things."

"Exactly, Director. Now, do you understand my concern? What do you suggest as our next steps to keep all important parties safe?"

"I believe it's time to call in a few favors. Let's start with the Little Rabbit."

21

DEVANI

I INHALED DEEPLY AND ADJUSTED THE CUFF ON MY WRIST.

In a few moments, I'd arrive at the headquarters of Maya Ratna Holdings and execute a plan months in the making.

Parts of me regretted not bringing Danika in sooner. Then, other parts wondered if knowing what I did now would have made a difference.

This was never supposed to be about me. Well, maybe not just me. But Papa. His money. His wealth. His mines.

My sole motivation for orchestrating this mission lay based on acquiring justice for Sam, giving him revenge against a father who took so much from him. Taking down the Circle of Ten and destroying my uncles, no matter how much I hated them, were only side benefits.

My safety, security, and future weren't even on the list of priorities.

Now, it seemed everything centered around my survival.

All the months Neil and I had spent listening to Joshi and Shah go on and on about us producing the next generation. About how Neil was as much Shah's child as Joshi's. In that case, the truth was more than fucked-up.

I'd ignored the constant talk of babies, thinking it was their way of trying to act all happy-family for the public. When they'd had a hidden agenda. Something I should have picked up on.

I knew better. I rarely missed clues.

They weren't the type to dote on a child, especially with how they'd raised their own children.

Why hadn't I delved deeper into their motives for a baby?

Too late to berate myself about mistakes, my focus needed to stay on the information Danika had uncovered using her Dark Web hacker skills. She'd uncovered a long-closed email account used to communicate to all of the men in the circle, which traced back communications to other accounts and then led to a giant paper trail.

Now I possessed, names, dates of meetings, agreements, terms, costs, collateral, and most of all, consequences.

Without Neil and I producing a child, the debt my uncles owed Joshi and Shah for the murder of my parents and brother would never be clear.

Just like a child had cleared Shah's debt to Joshi, the

deal my uncles had made required the same price, with me as the collateral they'd used for payment.

From the beginning, I'd been the bargaining chip for everything. I had the pedigree, the connections, and the money.

It finally made sense why my aunts had kept pushing Neil at me over the years. And also why they'd lost their shit when I told them I wasn't interested in him except as a friend.

If they'd only known, until Sam, I'd never planned to marry or have children.

This baby I carried had defied a birth-control method with almost a nonexistent failure record.

Never would I have believed I'd be a central piece in a breeding agreement. Yet, why was I surprised by any of this? Nineteen years in Solon taught me those with the image of saints could do things worse than the devil.

I set a hand over my stomach.

Now, I carried the wrong Shah son's child, and it had fucked up everyone's plans.

Good thing I knew how to protect myself.

"The queen needs to cool it with her ire. I can hear you grinding your teeth from over here." Sam watched me from his spot on the other side of the car bench seat. "Nothing is supposed to ruffle your feathers, remember? Cold as the diamonds in her mines and all that shit."

"I know how to do my job. You didn't have to tag along. This isn't my first rodeo."

With the threat to our child, and in turn to me, nothing

outside of a force of nature would have kept Sam away from my side.

I understood his fear and his need to protect me. He trained with the King security team regularly, so he wasn't a weakling. Still, he wasn't Solon and had no concept of what giving a girl some breathing room meant.

"I enjoy watching you work. Think of me as backup."

"I've managed countless assignments without you in tow. Also, Neil is more than capable of handling any unforeseen incidents. I've worked with him on and off since I was fifteen. He knows all my cues."

"Maybe. However, Neil's never handled this version of my wife before." The smirk on Sam's lips had me narrowing my eyes and ready to punch him. "The blood in her veins is no longer ice, so it's better if I'm around to ensure she doesn't kill someone prematurely."

"Like you?" I asked. "Pregnancy doesn't mean I don't have a functioning brain, Sam. I was running operations while you were still figuring out puberty."

"Yes, I remember, child assassin recruited at thirteen," he muttered and then added, "Do you even realize how fucked-up that whole situation was?"

Ignoring his question, I said, "Between my team ready to activate with a simple command, Neil ready to act in the room, and Dani and Noah feeding me info through the com-link, we have it covered. Plus, I'm armed to the teeth. You're going to be a distraction. This wasn't even part of the plan."

"Leave it alone, Devani." Sam's voice grew hard. "I'm

going in there with you. We agreed to do this together. That means a King is required to be at the table."

"A King *is* at the table, or did you forget about this?" I waved a finger with my platinum band back and forth.

The crease between his brow softened as a smile touched his lips. Reaching to his side, he captured my left hand, his own band reflecting in the sun's light.

"That's right." He rubbed his thumb over the stones in my ring. "The King finally captured the queen."

I rolled my eyes. "Possessive men are a turnoff."

"That's rich, coming from the woman who claimed me in a room full of New York's elite." He pulled me toward him, bringing my face to his.

I licked my lips, and immediately his pupils dilated as he followed the movement of my tongue. "You think too highly of yourself."

"Doesn't change the facts."

A moment before our mouths brushed, Noah's voice came through the transmitter hidden behind my earring. "Are you two going to continue your weird form of foreplay, or can we finish the assignment?"

"Let's finish this, Mr. Carter," I responded to Noah but kept my gaze on Sam.

He brushed a stray hair from my forehead and then pulled back, reaching for the door handle.

I scooted behind Sam.

Time to enter the very building where it all started. Where a group of fuckers had gathered and decided the fate of a little girl, where they'd plotted the deaths of an innocent man, woman, and child, where they'd organized to create a business designed to destroy the lives of countless women to create legacies for disgusting men like them.

As I stepped out in front of the steel-and-glass building, I gathered all my focus for the task ahead. The turmoil whirling inside me skated slowly to the back of my mind, and the training ingrained from the moment I'd accepted my role in Solon pushed forward.

No more emotions, no more worries. The only things that mattered were my end goals.

I was no longer Devani Patel, orphaned heiress to a multibillion-dollar fortune. In her place stood the Director of Solon North America, the assassin going by the alias Van, the woman known for using any means necessary to accomplish her mission.

Squaring my shoulders, I made my way to the doors of the building.

"Wow."

I glanced up at Sam. "Care to clarify that?"

"Don't think I've ever seen the transformation take place before. It's quite fascinating."

"I have no idea what you're referring to, Mr. King." I nodded to the doorman, who inclined his head as he waited for us to enter.

"Sure you don't, Highness. Interesting how fast your blood went from molten to arctic."

"I am who I am, Mr. King. You hitched yourself to my many different quirks and unique talents."

"That I did."

His palm grazed the curve of my lower waist and then flattened when he discovered the secret hidden under my clothes.

"You could have told me. I may not have acted like such a Neanderthal." His fingers ran along the stitching of my protective gear, going down my spine.

"I doubt that." I snorted. "For the record, all of my agents wear them in the field. And before you ask, mine is modified for my situation."

"Situation?"

Instead of answering him, I approached the head of security waiting to open the elevator set to take us to the executive floor.

"Is everyone settled inside the conference room, Tucker?"

"Yes, Ms. Patel. They are all waiting. A few of the attendees are agitated about your request."

"I appreciate your taking the brunt of the issues. Also, it's Mrs. King now."

Tucker's eyes widened, then shifted to Sam, who remained silent behind me.

"So the rumors are true."

"What, exactly, are the rumors?"

"That you gave up the company to marry Mr. King."

Oh, those rumors.

Ever since Sam and my relationship went public, all kinds of rumors had circulated about us. Everything from he'd seduced me away from Neil for my fortune to people believing I was going through a phase and I'd return to Neil.

The thought of Sam and me falling in love seemed unbelievable.

They'd eventually catch on that we were a permanent thing as everyone had with Jayna and Kir's relationship and Danika and Nik's.

"I haven't given up anything. Marriage changes nothing."

"Well, except her last name," Sam added.

Tucker's grin had me smiling. "Good to know."

He inserted a key into a panel, and the doors to the elevator opened.

Sam and I arrived outside the conference room less than two minutes later.

"Ready?" Sam asked.

"Absolutely." I touched my earring. "Keep monitoring and pass any information necessary."

"We got you, Van," Danika said. "Your tablet has all the information and will upload with additional updates as they come through."

Then Noah's voice came over the line. "Going silent in three, two, one."

I turned the doorknob, and immediately an onslaught of hate barreled toward me.

My uncles, Nishant, Naresh, and Hiren, sat together on one side of the large oval-shaped table. On the other side sat Ashok Shah and a few chairs from him, Arun Joshi and Neil.

Missing were Leonard Gustov and two other European Circle of Ten compatriots. All of whom were having a nice meditative sojourn in the underground cellars at the Sonnita Winery.

And, of course, the elusive Mr. Skylar Anton. As of this moment, he sat neck-deep in a fight with the Maldivian government for causing environmental damage when his yacht entered and then capsized after hitting rocky, shallow waters in a restricted nature preserve.

I felt no remorse or guilt over what had happened to any of those men. They deserved everything done to them and more. Solon's practices saved innocent lives, so the ends justified the means.

Maybe Solon had brainwashed me.

I scanned the room's periphery, counting the number of personal security scattered throughout the space.

Twelve. Actually eight. Four of them were my people posing as Neil's detail. They'd observe the players and only intervene if absolutely necessary.

"What is this all about, Devani?" Uncle Nishant demanded in English. "And why are we in this room?"

Because this is where you arranged to murder your brother.

I left the doors wide open and strode into the room with Sam behind me. Why not make it easier for the team when I gave the signal to extract the assholes?

"Hello, Uncle. It's nice to see you too. I'll answer your question in a moment. First, I'd like everyone to meet someone." Sam and I made our way to the open seats but remained standing.

"We know who he is." Ashok Shah scowled at Sam. "Are you here to gloat?"

"Gloating is for amateurs. I'm merely here as an assistant."

Assistant, my ass.

Keeping that thought to myself, I took a breath and prepared for whatever verbal assault Shah prepared to throw at Sam.

"It won't last. Her blood is too pure compared to yours. She'll come to her senses and pick someone worthy of her."

Sam set a hand on my back. "Maybe. But then again, your blood runs in my veins, and it's as tainted as it comes."

Okay, that was unexpected. Sam had never publicly acknowledged his paternity. And with the doors open, anyone who walked by could have heard him.

I glanced up at him. His eyes and face were completely void of any emotion.

However, when I turned my attention to Shah, his face showed his utter hatred, skin red, brow furrowed, and eyes full of rage.

"You aren't my son."

"That's true. I'm Arin King's son. In fact, I'm his Ruthless Heir, or haven't you read the headlines?"

"He was nothing but an interloper, just like you."

"Maybe I am." Sam shrugged. "It still doesn't change that I'm here."

Before Shah could continue with another jab, I spoke. "I'm sure everyone wants to get to the point of why I called this meeting. Let's begin."

"Start with my original question," Uncle Nishant demanded. "Why are we in here instead of the boardroom?"

I smirked. "I thought it appropriate to meet in the very room a group of men decided to arrange the future of a little girl and the demise of her parents and brother."

A beat of silence washed over the room, but it lasted only as long.

"What are you accusing us of?" my uncle Hiren asked, his anger rising. "Are you saying we had something to do with Rishaan's death?"

"You said it, not me."

"You have no proof, and this ridiculous gathering is a waste of time." Uncle Nishant attempted to rise from his seat but sat again when he noticed the tablet in my hand.

I pulled up all the various documents Danika had loaded onto the device, including one with all three of my uncles' signatures. The agreement to the marriage of one Devani Maya Patel to Neil Shuchen Joshi.

"Uncle, tell me, do you see the terms for the marriage and the child I would have to bear? Let me list them. Proof of death, requiring physical bodies. One hundred percent evidence of the execution of Rishaan Patel's will and transfer of assets."

"That proves nothing." Uncle Naresh finally decided to join the conversation.

"Did any of you question why four of your brethren are missing?" My attention shifted to Neil for a brief second, garnering a slight quirk to the corner of his lips, and then I focused on Arun Joshi. "A member of your group met with someone known as the Extractor, and after a bit of convincing, he agreed to cooperate with our investigation in exchange for his continuous standing in your hierarchy."

Then, I looked in Shah's direction and shook my head. "I made a late-night visit to your home recently and learned you were a very, very bad boy. You should know better than to have hidey holes in your office. A basement, a broom closet, or even a pantry are better places than your office. That's the first place people will search when looking for secrets."

Shah's face flashed with shock.

"We know everything. And you provided the evidence. Thank you for keeping such detailed notes on your activities."

"It won't stand up in any court, and it will ruin your family as much as it will mine."

I had no doubt if Shah could reach across the table and strangle me, he would.

"You forget, I don't care about my family's reputation. They sold me, remember?" I side-eyed my uncles. "Also, I'm not the type to wait for a court to dish out justice. This meeting was a setup. Get prepared for a very bleak future."

"Are you threatening us?" Uncle Nishant smacked his hand on the table. "Go ahead, little girl. Just because you have a King next to you doesn't give you any power."

I glanced up at Sam, who smirked at me. "I don't need a man to fight my battles. I'm more than capable of kicking your ass."

At my threat, all security shifted.

"In a few minutes, a group of travel coordinators will take you on a nice long vacation. If you're unlucky, you may meet the Extractor."

A throat cleared, and I met Neil's bored expression and then a roll-it-along motion of his fingers while bringing them across his neck.

Okay, then. Things had just gotten easier.

That was my signal that the recon team had relayed that everyone around us, excluding our men, had taken part in the Circle's business.

"I believe I need to move things along." Positioning my feet to maintain my balance, I said over my shoulder, "I'd suggest you get out of my way."

"Don't I get to participate?" Sam asked in an amused whisper. "I'm an excellent shot."

How had he figured out what I planned to do?

Knowing Sam's skill with a gun went beyond excellent, I relented. "Fine, the blues."

In the next second, from inside my suit jacket, I pulled out a pistol with a silencer. I disabled three of the eight security along the windows, while Sam handled the two wearing blue suits, and Neil took care of the three near him.

Shock washed over the faces of the men around the table, and the only sounds heard were those of the men dealing with bullet injuries.

With a nod from Neil, three of his team grabbed my uncles

and dragged them screaming from the room. At the same time, the remaining agent posing as security restrained Joshi in his chair with the weight of one heavy hand on his shoulder.

Almost as if in slow motion, Neil stalked in Shah's direction, anger blazing in his dark eyes. "Let's restart this conversation. Which of you fuckers wants to be next? How about you?"

"W-what are you doing?" Shah stammered. "Have you lost your mind? I've treated you as if you were my own son."

Fuck. That was the wrong thing to say.

Neil's grip tightened, and he adjusted his finger, ready to pull the trigger.

"Why don't we get some answers first?" Sam pushed down the weapon, pointing the barrel away from Shah's direction and to the ground. "Then, you can finish it."

Neil and Sam stared at each other, a war of emotions flowing between them. With the two brothers so close together and Shah in the background, there was no doubt the three of them shared some sort of relationship.

"He doesn't deserve to live. I will make him pay," Neil promised.

"Seems only fair." Sam continued to maintain his hold on the gun. "How about reminding him of everything he lost before you make it easy on him and put a bullet between his eyes?"

"Ten minutes, no more." Neil moved to the side. "My mother deserves justice from both of them."

"What have I done to you?" Shah continued to feign his innocence.

"You can drop the act, Shah." Sam kept his body between Neil and Shah. "It's over. You've lost. Accept it and deal with the consequences."

"I will never lose to a King."

I clenched my jaw and couldn't help but respond. "You've already lost. Jayna and Danika are now both Kings. Sam is a King. I'm carrying Sam's child. And most of all, the Kings helped the son you wanted but couldn't claim to destroy you."

"That child hasn't arrived yet."

Immediately, my senses fired, hearing the threat in his words.

The window shattered, and before I could duck, something hit me in the chest and abdomen, throwing me back. I collided with Sam right as Neil's body landed over both of ours.

22

SAM

MY HEART HAMMERED INTO MY CHEST AS MY MIND WHIRLED with thoughts of Devani and how I'd barely caught her before she slammed to the floor.

I held her to me, scanned the area, wanting to make sure the shooting stopped, and then shifted us to a nearby wall.

The bastard had planned this.

Neil rolled to his side and groaned. Then in the next second, he jumped up and shouted orders into a wrist communicator. "Tell me you have that fucker. Get him in the room, I'll deal with him personally. Find out what kind of rifle he had. And why the fuck wasn't anyone watching the radio tower?"

Devani eyes fluttered open.

"Sam. I told you I had it covered."

"Don't smile at me. I find nothing in this situation amusing." Laying her flat on the floor, I pulled her jacket and shirt open. "You're going to have some serious bruising, woman."

"It's par for the course in this business."

I touched all the spots where the metal plates held evidence of bullet impact.

My hands shook as I realized Shah had fucking set her up to die to keep me from having her.

He'd orchestrated the very thing I feared. I could have lost her.

"Hey." She grabbed my arm. "I'm okay. Just dazed. I'll be fine in a few minutes."

Ignoring her, I rose to my feet. Rage coursed through me as I readied to complete what I'd kept Neil from doing.

Erase Ashok Shah from existence.

Suddenly, I froze, unable to comprehend the sight before me.

Ashok Shah and Arun Joshi's bodies lay slumped on the floor, eyes open and hollow. Blood oozed from single bullet wounds to their foreheads. The placement of the entrance wounds was so perfect, so precise, the person taking the shots had either trained long and hard or ranked as a professional.

Then I focused on the shooter.

Smita Joshi.

She stood regal in the doorway of the conference room.

She held two pistols, one pointed toward her now dead husband and the other at her rapist.

In any other circumstance, the former model, with her flawless makeup, impeccably tailored clothes, and emotionless stance, would have looked like she posed for a clothing campaign.

"I've waited thirty-four years to do this," she whispered. "I'm free now."

A tremor shook her body, and she swayed.

Without thinking, I jumped up, running toward her. The adrenaline surge she'd just experienced would turn into a catastrophic crash within moments.

Neil and I reached her a second before her legs gave out. I grabbed her guns as Neil cradled his mother against him.

He crooned to her, "I've got you. It's over."

She buried her face into his chest as he brought her to a nearby chair and placed her in it.

Devani moved in beside me, holding out a towel. Without a word, I took the cloth, wrapped the firearms, and then placed them inside a bag she held open.

As I pulled my hand out of the satchel, our fingers lingered, and we stared at each other.

Everything over the last few months had led to this point, to an end we hadn't expected.

I could have lost her.

How the hell would I have survived without her?

"Your mom, Veda." Smita Joshi's voice broke the trance

between us, and reluctantly I shifted my attention away from Devani.

"She wasn't only meeting your grandparents that day. She was meeting me." A sob escaped her lips. "It's my fault she died."

A chill shot down my spine. Slowly, I moved in Smita's direction, only stopping when I was within her eyesight.

"Did you tamper with the bus?" I asked.

She shook her head.

"Then, you are not responsible."

The asshole on the floor had tampered with the bus. Shah had paid off the truck driver to run the red light. Shah had caused the wreck.

"I'm the one who sought her out."

I let her gather her thoughts, knowing whatever she wanted to say were things she'd kept hidden for decades.

"I knew about her. Arun and Ashok kept tabs on her, just in case she stood in the way of Ashok's marriage to Monica. It took years, but I waited. I waited until my boys and you were old enough to go to school before reaching out to her.

"We became friends, and together, we were going to tell Ashok's parents what their son was doing behind their backs. The Shahs were good people." A tear slipped down her face. "If I'd only thought to arrange for her transportation, she wouldn't have taken the bus. I should have known to cover my tracks better. I was so stupid."

"You can't think like that, Mum." Neil squeezed Smita's hand.

"He's right. You aren't responsible for the actions of monsters. I could never fault you for trying to find an escape from your prison. Neither would my mom."

Devani set a hand on my shoulder. "It's time to build a new, different life. One that you want."

Smita nodded and then whispered something to Neil. A few seconds later, he left with his mother.

"Sir, I believe it's time for all non-essential personnel and civilians to leave the area." Devani folded her arms and tapped her foot. "We have a cleanup team ready to sweep the area."

There was no use in demanding she tended to her own bruises or well-being.

She never gave an inch when in director mode.

"Is my wife kicking me out?"

I loved seeing that irritated crease form between her brows when I annoyed her.

"No, the Director of Solon North America is telling you to get lost."

"I hear you."

Just as I turned, in a voice only I could hear, she said, "We're both fine. You can stop worrying. I've had serious injuries before and survived. Getting shot with a vest on is nothing."

"Your attempts at reassurance need some work."

She shrugged. "At least I tried."

As I made my way to the doors, I caught sight of Shah's and Joshi's lifeless, still bodies.

All the humor from a moment before disappeared as

something I could only describe as a state of apathy washed over me. All the rage and hatred built in my system over the years no longer existed. In its place sat complete nothingness.

Stopping, I studied them.

These two men had caused so much chaos and pain. All for what? Power and money.

Especially Shah.

He'd destroyed so many lives to achieve his goals.

And in the end, he hadn't died by my hands, the son he'd thrown away, or by the one he'd created out of brutality, but by those of his victim.

As Lilly would say, Fate always possessed a sweet sense of justice.

If this wasn't justice, I wasn't sure what was.

A group of men and women dressed in black, carrying duffle bags of the same color, entered the room. With one last look, I put the demon who'd consumed so much of my history in the grave.

"ARE WE ALL IN AGREEMENT?" I ASKED JAYNA AND DANIKA. "Only sign if you are sure."

Less than two weeks after the incident at Maya Ratna Holdings, the three of us sat in the living room of my penthouse with an array of documents set before us. We were about to decide what to do with all of Shah International's assets.

As far as the public believed, Shah and Joshi had died while on a ski trip when Shah suffered a heart attack and lost control of their all-terrain vehicle. The news outlets reported that both men suffered life-threatening injuries and passed en route to the hospital.

It truly amazed me what Solon had managed to organize within hours of the two men's actual deaths.

"I'm sure." Danika rubbed her growing belly. "I thought I deserved a piece of the Shah inheritance. But the truth was, I didn't want Uncle to have it. Between Nik and me, this little one has more than enough."

"I tried to give it to you years ago. That should tell you enough," Jayna added. "Besides, according to the will, it doesn't belong to any of us in the first place."

"Then, we sign."

Fifteen minutes later, every asset under Shah International, including the ones Jayna and Danika had acquired to keep Shah in line while alive, had been transferred to Neil Shuchen Joshi, the eldest of Sara Shah's grandchildren.

"Now we wait." I checked my watch. "I give it an hour, max."

It took less than a half hour before security alerted me that Devani and a very irate Neil Joshi were on their way up to the penthouse.

The elevator doors barely opened when Neil charged in. "I don't want it."

Devani shifted into my sight behind Neil and shook her head, telling me without words that I was in for a fight.

"Too late." I lifted my tumbler of scotch to my lips, knowing exactly the rage he had to work through.

"I will burn it to the fucking ground."

"It belongs to you. Do what you want with it. I'll hand you the match if it makes you feel better."

"Why? I sold you that bastard Joshi's company for a fucking reason." He ran a frustrated hand through his hair. "Shah wasn't my father."

"Or mine. But the will states that the eldest gets everything. The rest of us oversee the company."

"Do you understand what you are handing over to me? I'm a complete stranger!"

"My wife trusts you. That's all I need to know."

"You have no clue. I could be just as bad as the monster whose blood runs in our veins. If you knew half the shit I've done."

"And if you knew what I did as a kid to survive the streets before Arin King found me, you'd feel the same way."

"What will you say if I give everything to Mia? She is the most innocent in all of this. If anyone deserves a fortune, it's her."

"Go ahead. It's your company, your empire. You see, the Kings don't work the way other families do. We don't need to share blood to be a unit. It's never about who has more. It's about survival and making sure everyone makes it."

"Meaning?"

"Mia is part of our unit now." Jayna stepped forward, her eyes trained on Neil, taking in every one of his features. "You want to give it to her. That's your right. You're family, so she's family. Simple as that."

"Nothing's that simple." Neil stared at her just as intently.

"It was with us," Devani added. "Why can't it be the same with them?"

"You tried to kill me the first time I met you. I hardly consider that simple."

I couldn't help but smile at the annoyance he directed at Devani.

"Sam wanted to kill you too. So you're ahead of the game." Devani's tone grew serious. "Neil, you can make it as complicated as you want. Whether you like it or not, you have family, and they are all Kings. Might as well get used to it."

Neil remained quiet, lost in thought. Then, after a few minutes, he looked between Jayna and me and released a deep breath before nodding.

"I hope one of you is a good mentor."

"Why is that?" I asked.

"Because a thirteen-year-old girl needs to learn how to run a billion-dollar company, and with the responsibilities associated with my new promotion, I won't have the time to help my sister."

I jerked my chin in Devani's direction as she cocked a hip and folded her arms across her body, giving me a death glare.

"I believe I have just the right person for the job. She

recently retired from a high-stress position and may need some volunteer opportunities to fill the time."

"I HAD A FEELING I'D FIND YOU HERE," I SAID AS I MADE MY way up the final steps leading into Devani's meditation room.

The woman took my breath away. She was utterly gorgeous.

She stood with her arms braced against the floor-to-ceiling windows. The lights of the New York City skyline at night illuminated the dark room and cast her in a glow.

"I like it up here."

"So do I." I moved toward her. "But probably for different reasons than yours."

Turning, she leaned her back against the glass. "Are you sure about that? I have some fond tension-relieving memories in here."

A wicked smile touched her lips, giving me visions of everything I wanted to do with that mouth.

"Would you like me to build you a room like this in our new place?"

We'd decided to move out of the city onto the same property where her parents' home once stood. No house existed on the land at the moment, but soon she'd get the home she always wanted, where she felt safe and not alone.

"Why don't I build a whole floor like this for myself in our new place?"

Of course, she'd counter with something like that.

"As long as it has all the finer features I prefer, I have no objections." I approached, caging her with my body.

She pressed her palms to my chest. "I'm sure we can work something out."

"In the meantime, we need to decide where we are living for the next however long."

"Is there a problem with our current arrangement?"

"No more sneaking around through passageways and private elevators. I've captured the Queen of Diamonds, and the world will know it."

"You actually believe that you've captured me, Mr. King?"

"I know I have. And if you try to escape, I'll lock you in a tower and throw away the key."

She narrowed her dark gaze and tilted her chin up. "Try putting me in a tower and see what happens to you."

I cupped her throat and squeezed.

Immediately, her eyes dilated as a moan escaped her lips.

Leaning forward until our mouths brushed, I asked, "Wouldn't this room qualify as a tower, Highness?"

Her fingers wrapped around my wrist but made no attempt to break my grip. "This room can't hold me. You, of all people, should know this."

"True. Then again, the last thing you want is your freedom when I'm around."

"You're awfully conceited."

"Why shouldn't I be? I've had a queen submit to me multiple times in this room."

"A queen doesn't submit to any man."

"I'm not just any man. I'm a King."

She lifted onto tiptoes and cupped my jaw. "That's right. Mine."

Want to see how Danika and Nik got their start? Begin the Street Kings Series with *Dangerous King*.

Or

Start a different series taking you into the indulgent world of Vegas with *Master of Sin*.

Signup for my newsletter to receive the epilogue to Devani and Sam's love story and to catch up on all of the King brothers - *Ruthless Mischief*.

The End

https://geni.us/dangerousking

I'm the one she should have stayed away from.

The thief, the hustler, the boy without a past or a future. A kid forged by the rules of the streets.

She sees into my darkest depths and doesn't blink an eye.

She's my dream, my peace from a place I can never escape.

Then one day, she's gone, whisked into a world I refuse to taint with my touch.

Fifteen years later, she's back in my life, needing a favor only I can provide.

The street rat she once knew is now king of an empire where every favor comes at a price.

A price she says she is more than willing to pay. But the cost is all of her...body, mind, and soul.

https://geni.us/MasterOfSin

IT WAS ALWAYS HIM...

The one I shouldn't want, shouldn't crave, the one who could destroy my carefully built life.

Hagen Lykaios was the essence of sin, indulgence, and danger - everything I knew to avoid.

All it took was one unexpected touch, and he consumed me, left me begging, needy, and hungry for more.

He said if I entered his world he would corrupt me, own me, and change all that I had ever known...and you know what? ***I went anyway.***

BOOKS BY SIENNA

Rules of Engagement

Rule Breaker

Rule Master

Rule Changer

Politics of Love

Celebrity

Senator

Commander

Gods of Vegas

Master of Sin

Master of Games

Master of Revenge

Master of Secrets

Master of Control

Master of Fortune

Sweetest Sin

Intrigued By Love

Hidden Truths (HEA Collective Exclusive)

Street Kings

Dangerous King

Vicious Prince

Deceptive Knight

Ruthless Heir

Collections

Reckless Rome (A Cocky Hero Club Novel)

Take Me To Bed (Limited Run Anthology - 2019)

Meet Me Under The Mistletoe (Limited Run Anthology - 2021)

Nightingale (A charity anthology in support of Ukraine) - (April 2022)

Darkly Ever After (An Organized Crime Anthology)

ABOUT THE AUTHOR

Inspired by her years working in corporate America, Sienna loves to serve up stories woven around confident and successful women who know what they want and how to get it, both in – and out – of the bedroom.

Her heroines are fresh, well-educated, and often find love and romance through atypical circumstances. Sienna treats her readers to enticing slices of hot romance infused with empowerment and indulgent satisfaction.

Sienna loves the life of travel and adventure. She plans to visit even the farthest corners of the world and delight in experiencing the variety of cultures along the way. When she isn't writing or traveling, Sienna is working on her "happily ever after" with her husband and children.

Sign up for her newsletter for notifications of releases, book sales, events, and so much more.
http://www.siennasnow.com/newsletter
contact@siennasnow.com

Lightning Source UK Ltd.
Milton Keynes UK
UKHW011317210223
417314UK00004BA/342